TABLE OF CONTENTS

Kashmir Jungle

It's the middle of the afternoon and blistering hot. Lord Stoker Mcleod leads an entourage of British soldiers, porters, an elephant, an Elephant Handler, and an American hunter named John Merritt. The elephant is pulling a giant rectangular shaped object, covered by a large blanket. The object is the size of the elephant pulling it. The year is 1897. The British have reigned over India since roughly 1760. First under the British East India Company, and after the Indian Rebellion of 1857, control was transferred directly to the British Crown.

The entourage are trekking through a thick Kashmiri jungle. They near their destination. The porters clear a path and the British soldiers scout for danger.

Lord Stoker (mid-50s) is a towering figure. 6’3”, handlebar moustache, and a barrel-chested bodybuilder. Along with being the richest man in the British empire, he’s also the most confident, and ferociously competitive. John Merritt (mid-40s) is a rugged looking man, 5’11”, tough as a nail, and battled-hardened. Merritt is a world-renowned hunter.

The entourage reach their destination, an open and clear area, the size of a football field.

As the majority of the expedition team establish a base camp, Mcleod, Merritt, and two British soldiers examine the perimeter of the open field.

JOHN MERRITT

You dumped a ton of money getting here. With the loot you gave me, I can buy a country.

LORD STOKER MCLEOD

(stern tone)

If you survive.

JOHN MERRITT

(sarcastically)

I've survived Africa. Hunted a dozen lions. Evaded 100 Apache Warriors. And this pretty thing from South Texas.

Lord Stoker lightly laughs.

JOHN MERRITT

I've been around and I've never heard of this.

LORD STOKER MCLEOD

There are many things many men do not know.

Stoker reaches into his satchel, pulls out a small journal, and hands it to Merritt.

JOHN MERRITT

What's this? A journal?

As he walks the perimeter, Merritt examines the journal.

LORD STOKER MCLEOD

It belonged to a British Captain. He was lost in this area after the second Anglo-Sikh war.

Merritt stops. Something in the journal catches his full attention. Lord Mcleod continues walking. After a brief period, Merritt chuckles and then resumes walking.

JOHN MERRITT

(yells out to Lord Stoker)

What makes you think the Captain wasn't a good story-teller?

Lord Stoker Mcleod ignores Merritt. Merritt catches up to Mcleod.

JOHN MERRITT

How much did you pay for this?

LORD STOKER MCLEOD

As much as I paid you.

JOHN MERRITT

I guess the Brits aren't as savvy with money after all?

LORD STOKER MCLEOD

To forsake without examination is foolish. To invest money without guarantee is just as.

JOHN MERRITT

Depends who you ask.

Lord Stoker lightly laughs.

JOHN MERRITT

Until I see it. I don't know. If this thing exists, with all the coin you have, why not send others here to do the work. What makes you think you'll make it back?

LORD STOKER MCLEOD

You, Merritt. Why else did I shower you in money?

JOHN MERRITT

For my charm. Maybe my good looks.

Mcleod again snickers. A short moment later, one of the British soldiers spots something moving behind the trees. At first the soldier ignores it, but after seeing something move for the second time, the soldier informs the team.

BRITISH SOLDIER

Something moves behind the trees. It looks... big.

The four stop and examine the area in question.

LORD STOKER MCLEOD

Well, shall we take a look. You two

(pointing at the two soldiers)

head in that direction.

(pointing to the right of the soldiers)

Merritt, with me.

The two groups enter the jungle at two separate locations. All cautiously walk through the thick jungle. Not too long in, two rifle shots are heard to the left of Stoker and Merritt. They run toward the sound of the shots.

As Mcleod and Merritt reach the spot, the two soldiers hover over a large body on the ground. They move closer and see A 10-FOOT TIGER on the ground, motionless. The tiger is dead.

The British soldiers and Mcleod admire the size of the creature. Yet, Merritt, alert, is looking about. He senses danger. In the trees, he catches a glimpse of TWO LARGE FIERCE BROWN EYES staring at them.

Merritt sees only the eyes. As it dawns on him, the large eyes disappear. Suddenly, we hear a FEROCIOUS ROAR that shakes the foliage.

Sihindi

An Indian woman, Sihindi (40s), with a serene face, is sitting on the ground and meditating by a stream.

She hears the roar. Her eyes open. Rifle Fire is heard. She quickly gets to her feet and runs toward the gunfire.

Sihindi is fit and athletic, and her familiarity with the jungle makes it easy for Sihindi to move through. She reaches the dead tiger. She hears a person scream. The shriek is coming from Lord Stoker Mcleod's base camp. She heads in that direction.

Sihindi reaches the camp, and to her horror, the camp is in shambles. All are dead but one British soldier, and he's seen running into the jungle. The soldier is cut and bloody.

The Train

William Mcleod is on a moving train to Peshwar, from Bombay. He's in his mid-twenties, six-feet tall, handsome, fit, and clean-shaven. William sits in a cabin with a Scottish businessman, Alan Studwick. Studwick is in his mid-thirties, short, thick, and with a thick black beard. Alan is a comedic character who constantly tries to entertain those around him. The two are playing chess and Alan waits for William to make his move.

ALAN STUDWICK

I first played this game with my grandfather. That old bastard. Tough as a nail. He established this company with one donkey. 75 years later, two ships haul Studwick spices. If plans unfold in Peshawar, I will have one more.

WILLIAM MCLEOD

Who are you meeting?

ALAN STUDWICK

The richest man to visit the lav.

William laughs and then moves his bishop to takes Alan's castle.

ALAN STUDWICK

Well, that settles the matter. It's time to deliver a Scottish whooping.

Alan gulps his glass of whiskey and quickly moves his queen to threaten William's king.

ALAN STUDWICK

Check.

WILLIAM MCLEOD

My grandfather was a Scotsman.

William moves his king forward. This exposes Alan's queen.

ALAN STUDWICK

(sarcastically)

He must have been the running type.

Alan moves another piece and leaves his queen exposed.

WILLIAM MCLEOD

(as William moves to take Alan's queen)

He was the conquering type. Checkmate.

ALAN STUDWICK

Arg.

Alan gets up.

ALAN STUDWICK

(as he walks out the cabin)

Time to drain the weasel.

William picks up a book resting beside him and opens it, but before he begins to read, William turns his head and looks out the window. William sees two boys running in the distance. One boy is chasing the other.

The scene reminds William of a time when he was twelve years old, with his friend, Tommy. Tommy too was twelve. The two are running through the streets of London. A store clerk chases them. Tommy has a bag in his hand. The two appear as if they live on the streets.

The two dodge through crowds of people and eventually turn onto a coming street. Tommy and William run down the street and then turn a corner. The store clerk is a short distance behind them.

Tommy and William turn onto the next street and then quickly turn into an alleyway. They run behind a stack of large boxes and watch the store clerk pass by the alleyway. They then make their way to the abandoned building across from where they hide. The two crawl through a broken window and into the building. They run up four flights of stairs and into a room with a broken table resting in the center.

Tommy carefully places the bag on the table. William anxiously awaits. Tommy opens the bag and pulls out two apples.

William snaps back to reality, as he hears the train's horn and feels the train jerk.

A large elephant rests on the train tracks. The train stops a few feet from the elephant. An elderly man stands before the elephant and instructs the elephant to stay put.

Alan Studwick, from a window in the lavatory, sees something he doesn’t like, a dozen armed men on horseback riding toward the train. Behind the horsemen are just as many armed men on foot. The armed men wear turbans and they look majestically ferocious. Alan rushes out of the lavatory and back to his cabin.

To Alan’s surprise, William is not there.

Robbery

William is on top of the train and crawls to a supply cabin. The armed men are also moving toward the supply cabin.

The armed men reach the supply cabin first and pry it open. The two British soldiers inside give-up without a fight. The armed men examine the crates stored in the cabin and take those containing rifles.

William watches as the armed men unload the cargo and then jumps from the train and tackles two of the robbers. The robbers William fights are rebel Singhs. A Singh is a member of the Khalsa. William renders one of the rebels unconscious, Manh Singh, but the other, Jang Singh, is as a boulder and a talented soldier. The two go back and forth. No one is gaining the upper-hand.

Through the cabin window, Alan Studwick sees William battling. He bolts out from the cabin and then out the train.

Alan rushes to where the two champions clash. He briefly hesitates and then tackles William's opponent. Yet, Jang is too strong and Alan's interference only disrupts William's flow and gives Jang an advantage. Jang knocks down Alan and then William, before mounting a horse and riding away. After a short distance, Jang stops and looks back. He remembers his unconscious colleague. He considers returning but as he does he sees William, standing as if he's about to face an oncoming assault, and behind him, a small British regiment emerging from the train. The captain of the regiment,

Captain Fleck, in a brave manner, runs and stands beside William. The regiment assembles behind the Captain. The rebels ride away.

CAPTAIN FLECK

(turns to William)

You... you... You are one lucky chap. Those were Singhs, you see. We saw the entire skirmish. You almost had him. Captain Fleck, at your service.

Captain Fleck holds out his right hand, as he twists the tip of his moustache with his left. William disappointingly looks at the Captain and reluctantly shakes his hand.

WILLIAM MCLEOD

What do you mean? From where? Why did you not try and stop them?

CAPTAIN FLECK

Ummm... ahhh... From there.

(he nervously points to the cabin that comes before the supply cabin)

The enemy. They are tricky. They locked the cabin door. All we could do was watch. We were stuck inside.

William can sense that the Captain is lying. The Captain can sense that William doesn't believe his story. Alan Studwick regains consciousness.

ALAN STUDWICK

(woozy)

I'll gie ye a skelpit lug. Bassa. Come back here.

William, laughing at Alan's gibberish, walks over to Alan and helps him up. The Captain follows William.

The British soldiers have the unconscious rebel surrounded, but no one is moving to restrain the rebel. The soldiers treat the rebel as a sleeping lion.

ALAN STUDWICK

You said you were on leave?

Captain Fleck gives William a look of surprise.

WILLIAM MCLEOD

(staring at Captain Fleck)

Captain William Mcleod. Under General York.

(William turns to Alan)

This is not my unit. My unit fights with me.

CAPTAIN FLECK

Yes. Well.

The Captain is searching for something to distract William. The Captain notices the soldiers and the rebel. The Captain rushes to them.

CAPTAIN FLECK

(overly stern)

Why is this man not in chains?

SOLDIER TONY

(Irish accent)

For the same reason we remained in the cabin.

The Captain, embarrassed, looks at William and then cautiously approaches the unconscious rebel.

CAPTAIN FLECK

Gibson, hand me the chains.

SOLDIER GIBSON

I don't have the chains. Murphy does.

CAPTAIN FLECK

Murphy, the chains.

SOLDIER GIBSON

He's in the train.

CAPTAIN FLECK

Why is he in the train?

SOLDIER GIBSON

He fell asleep waiting for the Singhs to go. I did not want to...

CAPTAIN FLECK

(angrily interrupts)

Gibson. Please, get me the chains.

Captain Fleck's Lieutenant, Ridge, walks to the Captain from the train. Soldier Gibson walks to the train to search for the chains.

LIEUTENANT RIDGE

Captain.

CAPTAIN FLECK

Yes.

LIEUTENANT RIDGE

All the rifles and ammo were taken.

WILLIAM MCLEOD

We can track the Rebels.

CAPTAIN FLECK

NO, no. There is no time.

WILLIAM MCLEOD

(staring at Captain Fleck)

They have British guns and ammo. Guns and ammunition they will use to kill British soldiers.

LIEUTENANT RIDGE

The train is not going anywhere. There is no conductor.

CAPTAIN FLECK

What do you mean?

LIEUTENANT RIDGE

He fled.

WILLIAM MCLEOD

Captain, gather your men.

CAPTAIN FLECK

Ah... I think it best we stay and safeguard the passengers. This is a ruthless country.

William doesn't waste time with the Captain. He quickly grabs the rifle from Fleck's hand and runs after the rebels. Alan, hesitantly, follows William. Gibson approaches Captain Fleck with the chains.

CAPTAIN FLECK

(as he chains the rebel, he yells out)

Think about this. The train might not be here when you return.

Outskirts of Peshawar

A middle-aged Cow-Herder herds his cows toward a pool of water. After the herd enter the pond, the man walks to a nearby tree, sits down under the shade, and proceeds to close his eyes. He is tired. Just as the man closes his eyes, he hears strange noises coming from the left of him. Then, out from the corner of his eye, he sees something crawling from out the bushes. It's the British soldier who fled Lord Stoker's base camp. The soldier is slowly crawling on his fours and making his way toward the Cow-Herder. He's in bad condition. He looks heavily dehydrated. The soldier makes eye contact with the Cow-Herder and then collapses. The Cow-Herder, afraid, runs toward Fort Lockhart.

The Forts

A hawk soars the sky over Fort Gullistan, Fort Saraghari, and Fort Lockhart. Located in the North-West Frontier Province, the traditional path most invaders travelled into India, these three forts are purposed to defend against foreign incursions. In particular, Afghan Tribal invasions. This pathway has seen many conquerors, from many lands, including Alexander the Macedonian.

All the forts are built in a square shape, accommodate thick and high walls, and rest on ridge tops. Fort Saraghari lay between Fort Gullistan and Fort Lockhart, two miles from each, and is the smaller of the three. Saraghari is a signalling station, designed to assist Lockhart and Saraghari communicate.

The hawk lands on a tree near Fort Lockhart and gazes over a group of British soldiers playing cricket. A crowd watches. Everyone is happy and enjoying the day. As the cricket game is played, in the background, the Cow-Herder runs to the nearest British soldier, who stands in the audience. The two converse and then walk to the nearest British officer. The three talk.

Wounded Soldier

The British soldiers who were playing cricket arrive where the wounded soldier lay. Most of the soldiers are in full uniform, while some are partially dressed in their cricket gear. They proceed to carry him back to Fort Lockhart.

BRITISH OFFICER - ROBERTS.

He requires water. Did you give him water?

COW-HERDER

Sir. No Sir.

BRITISH OFFICER - ROBERTS.

Why not? He's dying.

COW-HERDER

I was afraid.

BRITISH OFFICER - ROBERTS.

Of what?

COW-HERDER

If someone saw me giving him water, they might believe it poison. Within a day, all of Peshawar will think I killed a British soldier.

BRITISH OFFICER - ROBERTS.

What? That is ridiculous.

The Cow-Herder puts his head down and continues to walk.

COW-HERDER

No. This is the new India.

Punjabi Jungle

It's the afternoon. William and Alan track the rebels.

ALAN STUDWICK

William, why are we doing this?

WILLIAM MCLEOD

I know why I am. Why are you following me?

ALAN STUDWICK

Stupid.

(laughs)

But you are more stupid.

William laughs.

ALAN STUDWICK

You pursue the smashers of empires. Why do you think Captain Fluffy hid in the cabin. We are lucky to survive the first encounter.

WILLIAM MCLEOD

We will survive.

ALAN STUDWICK

My father was there, during the Anglo-Sikh wars. He saw firsthand. These men are not human. They are beasts in battle.

WILLIAM MCLEOD

Yet, we defeated them.

ALAN STUDWICK

Barely, and not on the field.

WILLIAM MCLEOD

What do you mean?

ALAN STUDWICK

The old trick. Bribe the leadership. A few of them were given gold and land. They betrayed their own people.

WILLIAM MCLEOD

These are tactics of war.

ALAN STUDWICK

Yes, but there is no honour in this. The Sikhs were no threat.

WILLIAM MCLEOD

What's done is done. Besides, I thought you said they were beasts?

ALAN STUDWICK

In battle.

WILLIAM MCLEOD

I tease Alan. I worked alongside many Singhs. I respect them. They saved the British in 57, during the Indian Mutiny. We're fortunate that so many sided with the British after their land was annex in 49. If they all rebelled, we would not be here today.

Alan is running awkwardly. William notices this.

WILLIAM MCLEOD

What is it?

ALAN STUDWICK

Something in my shoe.

William stops. Alan sits on a big boulder and takes off his shoe. William stares in the direction they were headed.

ALAN STUDWICK

Why did some Sikhs not join the British after the wars?

WILLIAM MCLEOD

Would you? Would I?

ALAN STUDWICK

Why did they all not rebel?

WILLIAM MCLEOD

The same reason they lost their empire. Trickery. A treaty was signed. Their empire is held in trust. After a capable Sikh leader is groomed, The Sikh Empire will be returned. The death of Ranjit Singh...

ALAN STUDWICK

(shaking the rock from his shoe)

The first Sikh Emperor. Every man dreamt of visiting his kingdom. No person went hungry, poverty was non-existent, and their military, the finest.

WILLIAM MCLEOD

After Ranjit died, disorder followed. Too many were concerned with fattening their own treasuries. The Sikh populace saw this. In particular, the members of the Khalsa, the Singhs.

ALAN STUDWICK

(as he puts on his shoe)

My father spoke of the Khalsa. Guru Gobind created this armed covenant to defend against Mughal insanity. The Mughals were on a warpath. The Singhs saved India. Did you know, not all Sikhs are Singh. I thought they all were.

WILLIAM MCLEOD

Khalsa is for those willing to fight and die for humanity. Any person from any faith may join. Once a person is initiated into the mystical

Khalsa, their surname name is erased and replaced. Singh if a man. Kaur if a woman.

Alan hops off the boulder. They commence their chase.

ALAN STUDWICK

Death. That is a problem.

WILLIAM MCLEOD

Battling the wicked in this world is like fighting a million titans. Death is a real outcome.

ALAN STUDWICK

Similar to the Templars. Too bad that scum Phillip destroyed them.

WILLIAM MCLEOD

(sarcastically)

Did you not know, the Knights Templars worshipped DEMONS!

They both laugh.

WILLIAM MCLEOD

And King Phillip owed them enough gold to fill the pyramid of Giza.

ALAN STUDWICK

If they were still around, do you think they would work with the Khalsa?

WILLIAM MCLEOD

I don't know. Probably not. If the Templars still existed, the Crown would pit them against the Khalsa. The Khalsa defeated the richest empire the world is yet to see, the Mughal Dynasty. And after those tyrants fell, they smashed the ferocious Afghanistanis. Together, the Templars and the Khalsa might topple all the kings and queens on the planet.

ALAN STUDWICK

In almost every battle, they also defeated the British.

WILLIAM MCLEOD

After the Sikh Empire fell, the Singhs decided it was better to work with the British than the existing Sikh leadership. The better of two evils I guess. Now these lions are kept at bay by a promise to return what was taken.

ALAN STUDWICK

Dangerous.

(short pause)

What if they realize? What then? They might destroy the British from within.

WILLIAM MCLEOD

We will bring their numbers down before this happens.

ALAN STUDWICK

What is it with rulers and righteous groups? The Mughal Emperor attempted to eliminate the Sikhs. They were hunted like wild beasts and almost decimated. But somehow, they survived. They retreated to the jungles and within a generation, the Singhs came back from the dead and decimated the Mughals.

WILLIAM MCLEOD

Battle of Muktsar. 1705. Forty-one battled a supposed one-million-man army, dispatched by the Mughal Emperor to kill Gobind. The forty-one forced a Mughal retreat and Guru Gobind walked away completely unharmed. The forty Singhs with him died fighting. There is something mystical about these lions.

William and Alan track the rebel Singhs to their camp.

WILLIAM MCLEOD

Here.

The two take cover a safe distance away. William is carefully examining the camp. Alan finds a comfortable spot to sit.

ALAN STUDWICK

William, the knowledge you have... where did you learn all this?

WILLIAM MCLEOD

Books.

(pause)

Too many. We will hit them at night.

ALAN STUDWICK

What do you see?

WILLIAM MCLEOD

This might be their main station. More than fighting men here. Children sit underneath the shade of a large tree and read. A Singh is painting. Another Singh is preparing food. Two ladies are sparring with wooden swords. Two Singhs are shooting arrows at a target, and they look as if they're competing. A Singh beats two drums and a lady, sitting beside him, plays a compact piano looking instrument. Another lady is sitting alone and meditating. The Singhs who raided our train stand about and talk. The Singh who knocked you down sits in a tent and counts our guns and ammo.

ALAN STUDWICK

So, what next?

WILLIAM MCLEOD

We wait until night, sneak in, set fire to the guns and ammo. Simple.

To learn more about the Khalsa, please review Appendix A.

Lord Stoker Mcleod's Base Camp

Sihindi is gathering dry grass and tree branches. She piles them in the center of the base camp. She then drags all the dead bodies to the pile. She sets the pile on fire and prays.

Boom

William and Alan are seen running from a massive explosion and into the jungle. Amid the explosions and confusion, Jang sees William.

William and Alan are hustling through the jungle, back to the train.

ALAN STUDWICK

(laughingly)

Without a scratch.

Alan trips and tumbles. William laughs.

WILLIAM MCLEOD

Tell that to the ground.

Alan laughs. William helps Alan back to his feet. They resume their getaway.

ALAN STUDWICK

This story will make me famous. Alan Studwick defeats a band of the most battle-hardened warriors in India.

(snickers)

The lads will buy me beer for a year.

WILLIAM MCLEOD

What will the dirt receive?

ALAN STUDWICK

What?

WILLIAM MCLEOD

You defeated the biggest and the ground took you down. So...

ALAN STUDWICK

Not funny William. Not a bit.

Alan trips William. William falls to the ground. Alan keeps running. William laughs, gets up, and resumes running.

ALAN STUDWICK

What? If you tell I fell, I tell you fell. So, Alan defeats an army of Singhs and...

(looks at William and gestures for him to continue the story)

And...

(Alan again gestures to William to continue the story)

WILLIAM MCLEOD

And Alan makes a clean getaway. Unscratched.

They both laugh. William gives Alan a friendly push.

Wait

Captain Fleck stands in front of the train and beside him is Lieutenant Ridge and the Conductor.

CAPTAIN FLECK

We waited long enough.

LIEUTENANT RIDGE

We can wait longer.

CAPTAIN FLECK

Dead bodies cannot return Lieutenant. The Singhs got them. I can feel it in my bones.

The Captain gestures all to enter the train. William and Alan are a short distance from the train, but the Captain cannot see them. The train slowly commences her journey.

ALAN STUDWICK

(yells out)

Ooohhhhhaaaa... WAIT. HERE.

WILLIAM MCLEOD

No use. They cannot hear or see you.

ALAN STUDWICK

What now?

WILLIAM MCLEOD

Find a spot to rest. We walk in the morning.

The Something

No creatures are heard. The only sound comes from something large moving fast through the jungle. The pace of this "something large" slows as it reaches the base of a mountain. It looks up at a ledge, approximately 20 feet from the ground. This "something", from a still position, jumps onto the ledge.

This "something large" proceeds to travel a trail that leads up the mountain. As it does, it's heard making light growling sounds as if angry. At the end of the trail is a cave.

The cave is doom shaped and the size of an average bedroom. The walls of the cave are smooth, and if a person did not know this was a cave, they might think it someone's home. A few books are stacked on top of each other, and several rectangular boxes are seen. In the corner of the cave Sihindi sits behind a lit candle. She is meditating. As she is, growling is heard. Sihindi opens her eyes.

Early Morning

William and Alan are asleep. William is having a nightmare. William's nightmare is vague and of his time with Tommy. In his nightmare, a vehicle rushes toward him. William wakes from his nightmare energized and in a sweat. He gets up and starts to gather his gear.

WILLIAM MCLEOD

Time to move. Wake up.

William throws Alan's shoe at Alan.

ALAN STUDWICK

(mumbles)

Five more minutes Maw. The chickens are telling me.

William looks at Alan and decides to mess with him a little.

WILLIAM MCLEOD

(in a female voice)

What are they telling you dear?

ALAN STUDWICK

About the gold... the gold under the bridge.

WILLIAM MCLEOD

(in a female voice)

Ow, gold. What will you do with the gold?

ALAN STUDWICK

(realizes that William is messing with him)

Mother. Come closer. I do not want the neighbor to hear.

William moves closer.

WILLIAM MCLEOD

(in a female voice)

Yes dear.

Alan hits William behind his knees and William falls.

WILLIAM MCLEOD

(in his normal voice)

That is no way to treat your mother.

The two laugh.

Infirmary

The wounded soldier rests on an infirmary bed. He is half unconscious and in pain. A doctor and a nurse stand by his side. General Thomas Andrews, commander of Fort Lockhart, walks into the infirmary. The General is in his late 50s, muscular, and of average height. The General's Secretary, Huckslee, follows him. The Secretary is a young and nerdy looking man. The General approaches the doctor.

GENERAL THOMAS ANDREWS

How is he? Can he speak?

WOUNDED SOLDIER

(slightly opens his eyes and turns to the General)

Dead. They are all dead.

GENERAL ANDREWS

(after a short pause, the General moves closer to the wounded soldier)

What happened son?

WOUNDED SOLDIER

(raises his hand and reaches for the General)

The... The... The Devil.

(the soldier is too weak; his arm falls; he passes out)

Hindu Temple (Ashram)

It is the late morning. Peshawar is a busy trading hub. Here, all different cultural groups interact.

Swami Faki, a Brahmin in his mid-forties, is lecturing a group of people inside an Ashram. Swami Faki is a well-spoken, short, and chubby man who wears expensive clothing. He typically behaves as if he knows it all.

SWAMI FAKI

The body is a tool and it houses the most powerful energy in the Universe. If one understands how to use this tool, he can harness this energy and project himself anywhere on this planet. There is no need for horses, ships, or trains.

(brief pause)

Thank you. This will be all.

As the Swami finishes his lecture, his assistant, Charan, who is also in his mid-forties but thin and short, comes to him and whispers something in his ear.

Lucy is in the audience. Lucy is in her early twenties and beautiful. She's an ambitious person who inspires to write a book. She is currently working on a book about her travels in India and India's mystical ways. Lucy is the daughter of General Andrews, yet, she is not your typical 19th Century high society lady. Lucy approaches the Brahmin and his assistant as they're about to exit the Ashram.

LUCY

Swami. Swami. May I have a minute of your time. I am...

SWAMI FAKI

(stops, turns around, and smiles)

Lucy Andrews. I understand you are writing a book about India's mystical ways. How may I help you?

LUCY

Yes. I would like to ask you a few questions.

SWAMI FAKI

Please do.

LUCY

Well, first, how did you know my name?

SWAMI FAKI

Why, I can read your mind, naturally.

(laughs)

You are the talk of Peshawar, Miss Andrews.

LUCY

What do you mean?

SWAMI FAKI

Look around. Do you see any other English ladies, and as attractive as yourself.

(short pause)

I leave for Fort Lockhart. If you wish to continue this conversation, you may accompany me.

Swami Faki and his assistant exit the Ashram and toward the Brahmin's car. Lucy follows. The car is the latest, greatest, and expensive.

LUCY

What takes you to Lockhart?

SWAMI FAKI

The wounded soldier.

LUCY

What soldier?

SWAMI FAKI

The one who survived the Devil.

LUCY

The Devil?

Charan opens the car door for Lucy and Swami Faki. The two enter the car. Charan takes a seat behind the wheel and commences the drive to Fort Lockhart.

SWAMI FAKI

(as the Swami rubs the car seat fabric)

Feel this.

Lucy rubs the fabric.

SWAMI FAKI

This is from France. This here

(pointing to the custom panels)

is from Italy. And see the hood ornament.

Lucy looks to a large gold sculpture of a lion's head, resting on the front tip of the car hood.

LUCY

A golden lion's head!

SWAMI FAKI

Sculptured by India's finest. It cost me as much as the car. Miss Andrews, there is no other car as this in the world. Not even your Queen can say she owns a better car.

LUCY

Is she not your Queen too?

SWAMI FAKI

I am my own queen, my own king. Peshawar is my kingdom. The people come to me for guidance, not your Queen. She... she knows this.

The car drives by Lieutenant Hughes and Captain Ragi. The two are on horseback and travelling in the same direction. Ragi is a Singh and, along with his British uniform, adorns the five Ks of the Khalsa. The three items that can be seen are a long sword, unshorn hair, and an iron bracelet. The other two items, a wooden comb and undergarment, cannot be seen. Ragi is a tough looking man about six-feet tall and he wears a turban. Hughes is in his mid-twenties, handsome, with dusty blonde hair, and shorter than Ragi. He too is wearing his uniform.

Ragi and Hughes are travelling back from a dangerous mission, on the outskirts of British territory. They were sent to gather information. The Tribal Afghanies are constantly challenging the British presence in the North-West Frontier Province. To fend off Afghan incursions, intelligence is vital.

Lucy sees Ragi. Lucy turns and slightly leans out of the car.

LUCY

(with a big smile she waves frantically)

RAGI!

Ragi sees Lucy and salutes her. Lucy sits back down and turns to Swami Faki.

LUCY

I love Ragi.

Swami Faki is envious that Lucy gives so much attention to Ragi.

SWAMI FAKI

Captain Ragi is just a soldier. A brute.

LUCY

Ragi is a great man. He saved my father, during an Afghanie raid. He once, by himself, fought twenty raiders to rescue a young girl the Afghans kidnapped. God knows what would be of her if not for Ragi. He's like an older brother. He even taught me how to meditate.

SWAMI FAKI

Yes. Yes. What is it that you wish to ask?

LUCY

This car.

SWAMI FAKI

My car? Your book is about mysticism and the great godmen of India.

LUCY

Do not holymen reject material things?

SWAMI FAKI

Times are changing Miss Andrews. Even Swamis must change to survive.

LUCY

Does God change?

SWAMI FAKI

This is a silly question. I thought you understood the ways of India.

LUCY

Captain Ragi believes God is unchanging.

SWAMI FAKI

(slightly grumpy)

Yes. God is unchanging.

LUCY

Does the path to God change, moment to moment?

SWAMI FAKI

No. Now please. I am a Master of Vedic knowledge. I studied the ancient ways for thirty years. In the whole of India, there is no person who knows as much as I. The answers to your questions a student can give.

LUCY

If God is unchanging and if the path to God is unchanging, why must a godman change?

Unable to answer, Swami Faki stares at Lucy. Lucy is looking forward and points.

LUCY

Oh, look, Lockhart.

The fort can be seen a short distance away.

LUCY

What did you mean the soldier survived the Devil?

SWAMI FAKI

Lord Stoker Mcleod's expedition is no more. The soldier is the only person to return. He reports that the Devil killed them all.

Lucy recognizes an opportunity. Lord Mcleod, the wealthiest man in the Empire was murdered. Everyone in England will want to know what happened. Perhaps she can write this story.

The vehicle reaches the fort. Lucy quickly jumps out and runs into the fort, past the guard. Swami Faki gets out and proceeds to walk through the gates, but is stopped by the guard.

GUARD

Name please.

SWAMI FAKI

The General knows me.

GUARD

Name please.

SWAMI FAKI

Swami Faki.

GUARD

(skims through the list of names on his clipboard)

I am sorry sir; I do not see your name?

SWAMI FAKI

This is ridiculous. The General knows me. Everyone knows me.

GUARD

I am sorry sir. I cannot allow you to pass.

SWAMI FAKI

Request the General please.

GUARD

I cannot leave this post until my partner returns.

SWAMI FAKI

When will he be back?

GUARD

Soon sir.

SWAMI FAKI

Soon. What is soon?

GUARD

Please sir, I ask you wait in your vehicle.

Swami Faki storms back to his vehicle, gets in, and sits.

Road to Fort Lockhart

Ragi and Hughes are casually riding their horses. They are close friends. They've seen a lot of combat together. Ragi has saved Hughes a few times. Hughes knows this and respects this. As they ride, in the distance, the Lieutenant sees an elderly man sitting under a tree and meditating.

LIEUTENANT HUGHES

What is it about Punjab? Everywhere you look, there is a person praying, singing, serving, worshipping, meditating.

MAJOR RAGI

Do not be fooled Lieutenant, most of them are showmen.

LIEUTENANT HUGHES

What about him?

The Lieutenant points to the man meditating in the distance. Ragi turns his horse in that direction. The Lieutenant follows lead.

MAJOR RAGI

Let's take a look.

The man meditating notices the two riding toward him. He calmly reaches for a rifle hidden underneath the blanket he sits on. With his hand on the rifle, he considers firing at Ragi and Hughes. He decides not to, and instead, as Ragi and Hughes get close, he runs in the opposite direction and toward the tree line. The Major and the Lieutenant pursue.

As the two near the man, the man opens fire. Hughes's horse reacts as if shot and Hughes falls. Ragi continues to pursue.

The man quickly reaches six armed men, who appear to be with him. They all fire at Ragi. Ragi dismounts and takes cover. Ragi is cornered. Ragi is unable to fire back. If he breaks cover, he’s sure to be shot. It doesn't look good.

Suddenly, rifle fire is heard coming from the right of the men. One man is hit with a bullet and wounded. A few moments later, rifle fire is heard coming from the back of the men. Another man is hit and he too is wounded. The men do not know who's firing or how many rifles are pointing at them. Rifle fire is again heard from the right of the men. Ragi also unloads his ammo. This time, the men mount their horses and retreat. As they do, they carry the wounded with them.

Fort Lockhart

Lucy, searching for her father, runs into the building that houses the General's office. She doesn't see him and runs out.

Lucy sees a soldier in the courtyard.

LUCY

Have you seen the General?

BRITISH SOLDIER

No, I'm sorry Miss Andrews.

For a better view, Lucy climbs to the top of a fort wall. Lucy looks about the fort but doesn't see the General. She's frustrated. Then she hears her father.

GENERAL ANDREWS

Lucy. What are you doing up there?

Lucy hears the General's but can't identify his location.

GENERAL ANDREWS

Child, turn around.

Lucy turns around and sees the General standing outside the fort. He is instructing a group of British soldiers. Lucy is excited to finally find her father.

LUCY

(yells out)

Do not move. I will be right down.

Lucy climbs down and runs through the fort and out the main gate.

The General sees Lucy coming and wraps up his conversation with a salute. The soldiers salute back. The General walks toward Lucy. The soldiers remain.

GENERAL ANDREWS

Lucy, what is it?

LUCY

Lord Stoker Mcleod is missing. Possibly dead. I want the story.

GENERAL ANDREWS

What? Where did you hear this from?

LUCY

Swami Faki.

GENERAL ANDREWS

(murmurs to self)

How did he find out so quickly?

LUCY

Have you sent men looking for him yet?

GENERAL ANDREWS

No.

LUCY

(relieved)

Good. I need time to prepare. Father, this is my opportunity.

GENERAL ANDREWS

To achieve what? And what do you need to prepare for?

LUCY

For everyone to read my words. My thoughts. And to accompany the rescue mission.

GENERAL ANDREWS

You agreed that if I allow you to work on your current book, you will pursue no other nonsense. I'm tired of arguing with you. This is not the duty of someone as yourself. It is time to think about marriage Lucy... making a family.

The General walks toward the fort's main gate. Lucy follows.

LUCY

I will. One day. Just not now.

GENERAL ANDREWS

Sooner is better than later.

LUCY

Please Father, just this one thing.

GENERAL ANDREWS

No more Lucy. And you honestly expect me to allow you to trek through the jungles. I do not want to hear anymore.

LUCY

Why do you treat me as if I might break at the first sight of danger?

The General chuckles. As the General and Lucy near the main gate, Swami Faki, still sitting in his car, sees them. He exits his vehicle and quickly walks to the General.

SWAMI FAKI

General.

GENERAL ANDREWS

(as he walks)

Swami. How may I help you?

The General does not lose stride and continues his walk into the fort. Lucy and the Swami follow.

SWAMI FAKI

I must see the survivor.

GENERAL ANDREWS

How do you know of him?

SWAMI FAKI

The Cow-Herder.

GENERAL ANDREWS

Why must you see him?

SWAMI FAKI

To hear firsthand what he saw.

GENERAL ANDREWS

What does it matter to you?

SWAMI FAKI

The safety of the people, what else.

Train Tracks

William and Alan are walking along the tracks. They've walked under the hot sun for some time.

ALAN STUDWICK

No more. I need rest.

WILLIAM MCLEOD

(points to the train station ahead)

There.

William and Alan reach the nearest train station. The train that abandoned them is here and under repair. The Captain and his regiment stand about the station.

CAPTAIN FLECK

How much longer until repairs are complete?

LIEUTENANT RIDGE

The engineers are finishing up now.

William walks through the regiment and toward Captain Fleck. William punches the Captain square in the face. The other British soldiers tackle William. William fights them all. William delivers many hits and receives hits. Alan is also in the tussle and takes blows to the body and face. As a few soldiers hold William, William is hit unconscious.

Custody

William wakes to discover his hands and feet tied. He and Alan are under guard. They are back on the train and heading toward Peshawar. But this time, William and Alan are held captive in the supply cabin. The Singh rebel is in the same cabin and also in custody.

WILLIAM MCLEOD

Where is the Captain?

BRITISH SOLDIER - GUARD 1

(sarcastically)

His face required rest.

ALAN STUDWICK

So does mine?

BRITISH SOLDIER - GUARD 2

That was me.

(smiles)

William looks at the second British Guard. This guard has a nasty black-eye. William points to his own eye and then Guard 2's eye, to signal that he's referring to Guard 2's black-eye.

WILLIAM MCLEOD

That was me.

Guard 2's smile turns into a stern look. The cabin is silent. Then, suddenly, everyone bursts into laughter.

ALAN STUDWICK

The Captain left use behind. Why?

BRITISH SOLDIER - GUARD 1

He thought you two were dead.

ALAN STUDWICK

What? Why?

BRITISH SOLDIER - GUARD 2

The same reason the Captain hid in the cabin.

ALAN STUDWICK

Ah... Fluffy.

Captain Fleck bursts into the cabin.

ALAN STUDWICK

Fluffy!

Captain Fleck confusingly looks at Alan.

CAPTAIN FLECK

General Andrews will decide what to do with you. You should know, striking a British soldier is a serious offense.

ALAN STUDWICK

You are a serious offense Fluffy.

Everyone in the cabin, excluding Fleck, snickers. After a short stare at Alan, Fleck turns his attention to William.

WILLIAM MCLEOD

Untie me.

CAPTAIN FLECK

The General will decide.

WILLIAM MCLEOD

You are a coward Fluffy.

Lieutenant Ridge enters the cabin.

LIEUTENANT RIDGE

Sir. Peshawar.

Captain Fleck's attention again turns to William.

CAPTAIN FLECK

(smugly)

Prepare the prisoners.

The train approaches the station. The train is filled to the hilt with patrons. The passengers hop off the very moment the train stops. The British soldiers exit with William, Alan, and the Singh rebel in custody.

Tristan Jacob, Lord Stoker Mcleod's Assistant, stands at a counter, waiting for a parcel. He thinks he sees William through the window. Tristan is in his mid-forties, short, wears broken glasses taped together at the center, and is dressed in a three-piece suit.

The British soldiers, with the prisoners, travel to Fort Lockhart. Tristan, uncertain that it's William, follows. After a few moments of examining William, Tristan is sure it's him.

TRISTAN JACOBS

William. William.

WILLIAM MCLEOD

(looks about and sees Tristan)

Tristan.

(laughs in joy)

Tristan waves and runs to William.

TRISTAN JACOBS

What is this?

A British soldier stops Tristan. The remainder continue to move forward.

WILLIAM MCLEOD

Perhaps now is not a good time. The next time we meet, I will tell you everything.

BRITISH SOLDIER

Sir. I must ask you to back away. These men are in custody.

TRISTAN JACOBS

Where are you taking them?

BRITISH SOLDIER

Fort Lockhart. Now...

(gestures to Tristan to leave)

Tristan runs in the direction of his horse.

ALAN STUDWICK

Who is he?

WILLIAM MCLEOD

An old friend.

As Tristan is about to get on his horse, he recalls the parcel, and rushes inside the train station. A few moments later, with package in hand, he gets onto his horse and rides toward the Mcleod home.

Evidence

Tristan reaches the Mcleod home and heads straight into the study. Tristan rummages through the desk drawers. He finds what he's looking for. It looks like a rectangular piece of paper. Tristan then rushes out of the study, out the home, and mounts his horse.

Detention Center

William, Alan, and the rebel are ushered into their prison cells, in Fort Lockhart. The Fort Lockhart Detention Center is small, clean, and holds 6 cells. 3 cells on each side. William is placed in the center cell on one side. Alan is escorted to the cell left of William. The rebel is shoved into the cell across William's.

The General's Office

General Andrews, Lucy, and the Brahmin sit in the General's office. The General is behind his desk, Lucy sits to the right of the desk, and Swami Faki sits across the desk from the General.

SWAMI FAKI

I would like to see the wounded soldier?

GENERAL ANDREWS

He requires his rest. Perhaps in a few days.

SWAMI FAKI

A few days might be too late. The people must know now. If a demon roams near by...

GENERAL ANDREWS

Do not believe this nonsense.

SWAMI FAKI

Nonsense demons are not General. Now, please, allow me to speak to him. Or do you prefer all of Peshawar come here to ask?

GENERAL ANDREWS

How is it that all of Peshawar knows of this missing expedition? The soldier was found yesterday.

SWAMI FAKI

This is the new India General. Gossip loves tragedy, follies, suffering, and demons. Give it a month, all of India will know.

Tristan reaches Fort Lockhart's main gate. He dismounts and approaches the gate guard. He speaks to the guard and the guard permits him to enter.

Tristan runs into the building housing the General's office.

HUCKSLEE

Tristan. Good to see you. What brings you here?

TRISTAN JACOBS

Huckslee, my friend, I need to speak to the General.

HUCKSLEE

Yes, of course.

The General's Secretary knocks on the door and enters the General's office. He quickly returns and stands at the door, and gestures Tristan to enter.

GENERAL ANDREWS

Tristan, your timing is auspicious.

TRISTAN JACOBS

General, I am sorry to trouble you.

GENERAL ANDREWS

It is me who might be troubling you.

TRISTAN JACOBS

(as he hands the General the item, a picture)

General. I require your help.

Freedom

ALAN STUDWICK

(with his head down)

My third ship. William, my third ship. I see it sinking.

William laughs.

WILLIAM MCLEOD

Who were you to meet?

ALAN STUDWICK

Lord Stoker Mcleod.

WILLIAM MCLEOD

Ah, yes. The richest man to visit the lav.

Alan laughs.

ALAN STUDWICK

Men like him wait not for men as me. This was my one chance.

WILLIAM MCLEOD

The Lord will understand.

ALAN STUDWICK

These people do not care to understand. We are pawns to them. The world is their chessboard. He will find another pawn.

WILLIAM MCLEOD

These people?

ALAN STUDWICK

The super wealthy. The rulers. The demi-gods on Earth.

WILLIAM MCLEOD

They are more human than you might think.

The door to the Detention Center opens. General Andrews, Huckslee, the guard, and Tristan enter. The General walks to the cell. He looks at the picture and then William.

GENERAL ANDREWS

William Mcleod. This is no place for a man such as yourself.

In the background, Alan, puzzled, looks to William.

ALAN STUDWICK

Your father is Lord Stoker Mcleod.

(laughs)

Why did you keep this from me?

WILLIAM MCLEOD

You did not ask.

GENERAL ANDREWS

I understand you managed to destroy the stolen guns and ammunition. Well done.

General Andrews extends his hand and the guard gives the General the keys to the cell. The General opens the cell door.

Stoker's Son

Lucy and the Brahmin still sit in the General's office.

LUCY

During your lecture, you spoke about India's ancient past, flying machines, travelling to other planets, men living to one-thousand, as if you channeled Jules Verne.

Swami Faki laughs.

SWAMI FAKI

The truth is much more fantastical than his imagination. India's past is older than you know, and far more advanced than your boarding schools teach. They fear the truth might nullify your attitude of supremacy. Without this mind-state, how many British would have the nerve they do. Without this attitude, there might not be a British Empire.

(short pause)

India once ruled the entire world Miss Andrews. The Indian blood is still on every continent. What is it that you ask?

LUCY

Do you believe the stories you tell?

SWAMI FAKI

Of course. Astral travel, long-life, flying machines, this was all so. There were three types of flying machines, Vimanas. Each served a unique purpose. One transported a person to the stars. Another from one end of this planet to the next. And the third carried a person to where the demi-gods live. These Vimanas were either destroyed or hidden, in the previous Yug, to prevent the men of today from using these machines for evil.

LUCY

Where did you learn this from, and what is a Yug?

SWAMI FAKI

There are four Yugs, or epoches, that the solar system cycles through. Each epoch facilitates specific cosmic forces. These forces influence earthly activity. Currently, we are in the worst of these Yugs and the cosmic forces influence the darker aspects. For this reason, the world is in chaos - war, poverty, illiteracy, pollution, and spiritual ignorance are rampant.

(brief pause)

As for where I gained this wisdom. India is a storehouse of knowledge. Indians were writing books and recording history over 5 000 years ago.

LUCY

These books survived this long?

SWAMI FAKI

Yes, and they will survive another 5 000 years. My family alone cares for over 1000 books.

LUCY

Can I see this collection?

SWAMI FAKI

Only the family is permitted to study them. For more than 2000 years, father to son, this knowledge has travelled.

LUCY

Why the exclusion?

SWAMI FAKI

The knowledge is very difficult to understand. God has chosen my family Miss Andrews. We relay the teachings to the people.

LUCY

Yet, you managed to learn them, and as did your father, his father, his father's father. What makes other people less capable of understanding?

The General, Tristan, William, and Alan enter the General's office.

GENERAL ANDREWS

Mr. Faki. I must cut our time short.

SWAMI FAKI

General, the soldier.

GENERAL ANDREWS

Tomorrow will be better Mr. Faki. Lucy, please show Mr. Faki to his car.

Lucy gets up and walks to the door.

LUCY

Follow me Swami.

Lucy exits and Swami Faki gets up.

SWAMI FAKI

General, tomorrow might be too late.

GENERAL ANDREWS

Have a safe drive Swami.

SWAMI FAKI

Yes. Of course.

Swami Faki exits the office.

GENERAL ANDREWS

This matter involving Captain Fleck. I'll speak with him. In the meantime, I have something to tell you.

(short pause)

Son, your father and his expedition are missing.

WILLIAM MCLEOD

Missing?

WILLIAM MCLEOD

(William looks at Tristan)

Tristan?

TRISTAN JACOBS

I'm hearing of this for the first time. It is true that your father is behind schedule.

WILLIAM MCLEOD

It happens. This does not mean anything but that he is late.

GENERAL ANDREWS

There is a survivor. He is suggesting that your father's expedition is no more.

WILLIAM MCLEOD

Where is he? I must speak with him.

GENERAL ANDREWS

That will do you no good. He is not himself.

WILLIAM MCLEOD

He must know more. Tristan, where is the infirmary?

Tristan, confused and on the spot, shrugs his shoulders.

WILLIAM MCLEOD

General, please, you suggest my father might be dead, and this is all you have.

GENERAL ANDREWS

We do not know what occurred. All we know is that your father's expedition is 12 days late. A wounded soldier rests in the infirmary. He witnessed something horrendous. As soon as Major Ragi returns, we will organize a fact-finding expedition.

WILLIAM MCLEOD

When will this be?

GENERAL ANDREWS

Soon.

William gets up, salutes the General, and leaves the office. Tristan and Alan follow.

Sneaky

Lucy and the Swami are nearing the main gate.

SWAMI FAKI

Have you spoken to the soldier yet?

LUCY

No.

SWAMI FAKI

This might be a good time.

The Swami quickly changes direction and heads for the infirmary.

LUCY

Swami. SWAMI.

The Swami ignores her and continues walking. Lucy catches up.

LUCY

Swami, where are you going?

The Swami ignores her. He reaches the infirmary and enters. Swami immediately looks for the soldier. Lucy enters the room soon after.

LUCY

This is not a good idea. The General will not be happy.

SWAMI FAKI

The people's safety is at hand.

A nurse is cleaning. She sees the two and walks to them.

NURSE

Lucy.

The two embrace each other.

NURSE

What brings you here?

Lucy looks over to the soldier. Swami Faki is by the soldier's side. The Swami realizes that the soldier is sleeping. Beside the bed is a table, where two metal containers sit. The Swami slides one container off the table. The container hits the ground and bounces about. The wounded soldier suddenly wakes from the noise. The Nurse and Lucy rush to the wounded soldier's bedside. The Nurse checks on the soldier.

NURSE

Sir. What happened?

Swami Faki shrugs his shoulders. Lucy knows what happened and stares at the Brahmin.

SWAMI FAKI

Soldier, what did you see?

WOUNDED SOLDIER

General. The Devil... killed them all.

LUCY

(addresses the soldier)

This is not the General. This is...

Before Lucy can finish her sentence, the wounded soldier again falls unconscious.

SWAMI FAKI

Soldier. Soldier.

NURSE

It is no use sir. He requires rest.

SWAMI FAKI

What else did he say?

NURSE

Sir. This is a question for the General.

LUCY

Tomorrow will be a better day Swami.

The Swami, frustrated, exits the infirmary.

Stables

Ragi and Hughes ride toward Fort Lockhart. They are hungry, tired, and dirty. The Swami drives past the two.

LIEUTENANT HUGHES

Before or after? When would you like to debrief the General?

Major Ragi gestures as if he is sniffing the Lieutenant. Then he sniffs himself.

MAJOR RAGI

Perhaps after a bath.

They both laugh, as they reach the main gate to the Fort. They proceed to ride to the stables.

Ragi and Hughes dismount and secure their horses.

LIEUTENANT HUGHES

You know I saved you, right. I hit them from the right then the back. It was perfect.

MAJOR RAGI

Nine more and we might be square.

LIEUTENANT HUGHES

Remember that scuffle in the Khyber Pass. I thought we were done for.

MAJOR RAGI

You think that every time.

LIEUTENANT HUGHES

There were TEN-THOUSAND of them and two of us!

MAJOR RAGI

What are numbers when the fight is righteous. If the body dies, so be it. The soul lives forever.

LIEUTENANT HUGHES

Ragi, you are a renaissance man. Last week you were painting a portrait. I've heard you play that large violin instrument. You can debate the wisest scholars, and now a poet.

MAJOR RAGI

Esraj.

LIEUTENANT HUGHES

What?

MAJOR RAGI

Esraj is the violin like musical instrument, and I am far from a renaissance man.

LIEUTENANT HUGHES

And humble.

Ragi laughs.

LIEUTENANT HUGHES

Before coming here, I believed only Europeans understood music, art, writing, philosophy. It took me two years to appreciate that Punjab is advanced in these things too.

MAJOR RAGI

"Was" might be a better word. The artistic and scholarly half of Punjab is ill. Too many invasions. Too much destruction.

LIEUTENANT HUGHES

Punjab is now a part of the Empire, thus, what the British are best at, Punjab is best at.

Major Ragi remains silent.

Nightmares

William, Alan, and Tristan converse outside the building to the General's office.

TRISTAN JACOBS

This is not a good idea. The jungle is a dangerous place and night is nearing. William, you are tough. But. Perhaps wait.

ALAN STUDWICK

Wait for the General to organize his people William. I will come with you.

WILLIAM MCLEOD

This might take days. Maybe weeks. My father needs me now.

TRISTAN JACOBS

It will not take long to assemble a search party.

William quickly walks toward the General's office.

TRISTAN JACOBS

Where are you going?

WILLIAM MCLEOD

To talk to the General.

William walks into the building.

ALAN STUDWICK

Does that man not rest?

TRISTAN JACOBS

His curse.

ALAN STUDWICK

I know a man, for 2 pounds, he can lift any curse.

Tristan laughs.

TRISTAN JACOBS

It is not a hex. The hero he plays is the hero William thinks Tommy would be.

(short pause)

When William was twelve, his mother passed away suddenly. Lord Mcleod was overseas. All the House-Hands were new. William was alone.

That night, while William was staring out his bedroom window, he saw something, an apparition perhaps, standing outside the front gate, that resembled his mother. William went to investigate.

As William neared the gate, the apparition disappeared, and William walked out onto the street searching for what he saw.

William walked for an hour searching, before he tripped into a puddle of muddy water and knocked himself unconscious.

When he woke, he didn't know where he was, and because he looked filthy, no one would help him. They dismissed him as a street kid.

That night, as William was sitting in an alleyway, curled up, and crying. Tommy, from behind several large cargo boxes, walked to William and befriended William.

Tommy was a street kid but a big dreamer. He desired to become a soldier and help the Queen save the world. But one day, while crossing a busy street, William fell, as an automobile was approaching, and Tommy pushed William out of the way.

(short pause)

Sadly, Tommy was hit, and William feels responsible for Tommy's death. William lives like Tommy might.

William exits the building.

TRISTAN JACOBS

Well... are you willing to wait?

WILLIAM MCLEOD

For now.

TRISTAN JACOBS

Okay. Great. Let me show you your home.

Tristan walks to his horse and the other two follow. Tristan then turns to the two.

TRISTAN JACOBS

I only have one horse. Peshawar is 30 minutes from here.

ALAN STUDWICK

Perhaps the General has a horse or two to spare?

TRISTAN JACOBS

They are short on everything. William, you can ride my horse.

WILLIAM MCLEOD

Thank you for the offer but Alan and I will walk. It is only fair.

ALAN STUDWICK

Ummm. Alan prefers the horse. You two walk.

They all laugh. Tristan gestures Alan to ride the horse.

Bath Time

Ragi and Hughes are sitting in tubs of water. They are laughing. The Major gets out of the tub and wraps a towel around his waist. The Major is in peak physical form.

MAJOR RAGI

Prayer Lieutenant?

LIEUTENANT HUGHES

Ummm... you know exactly what happens every time I try. I am yet to understand the art. How do you manage?

MAJOR RAGI

Childhood habit. Good teachers.

(pause)

Meet me at the General's office in one hour.

The lieutenant nods his head. The Major exits the bath area. The lieutenant proceeds to submerge himself under the water.

A Man's World

The General is sitting behind his desk and reading a journal. Lucy enters the General's office.

GENERAL ANDREWS

Lucy, what brings you back?

LUCY

Oh, I miss you father.

GENERAL ANDREWS

(sarcastically)

Do you now.

LUCY

Yes. And I want you to know how much I love you.

General Andrews laughs lightly.

GENERAL ANDREWS

Anything else.

LUCY

And just being your daughter, makes me the luckiest daughter in all of England.

GENERAL ANDREWS

Just England.

LUCY

Yes. But this can change.

GENERAL ANDREWS

Oooo can it. Let me guess, if I allow you to investigate the Lord's whereabouts.

LUCY

That might do it.

GENERAL ANDREWS

(looks back at the journal)

Well, luckiest daughter, I have work to do.

LUCY

And.

GENERAL ANDREWS

And no. The answer is still no.

LUCY

Urrg.

GENERAL ANDREWS

Are you still the luckiest?

Lucy, angry, storms out of the office.

LUCY

(as she exits the office)

What do you think.

General Andrews laughs lightly.

Lucy angrily walks about in the courtyard, and as she turns a corner, she nearly collides with Ragi.

LUCY

Ooo.

MAJOR RAGI

Lucy. It is good to see you.

LUCY

You too Ragi.

MAJOR RAGI

How does the book progress?

LUCY

Who cares. No one cares.

MAJOR RAGI

What is this about?

LUCY

Men. Women.

Lucy starts to cry. She hugs Ragi.

LUCY

I am sorry Ragi. It is not you.

MAJOR RAGI

Did someone hurt you?

LUCY

The world hurts me.

Lucy's crying grows heavier.

MAJOR RAGI

(short pause)

Come with me.

Ragi continues to walk. Lucy follows.

LUCY

Where to?

MAJOR RAGI

Prayer. Meditation. Song. Forget about your worries for now. Get back to them after. Perhaps a solution will come to you.

Tougher than Tigers

It's a clear and beautiful night sky, riddled with specks of shiny dots (stars). Under this beautiful night sky lurk two vicious and large tigers. These beasts are tactfully moving toward their prey, resting behind several tall bushes. A tiger pounces over the bushes. The second tiger rushes around the bushes and attacks. Mighty roars are heard. Then suddenly, nothing. After a moment of silence, one by one, the two tigers are seen flying back over the tall bushes, as if someone picked them up and threw them. They hit the ground and slide a short distance. Both tigers are motionless and there's no blood or wounds. It's as if their necks were snapped. A loud roar, from “the something" is heard.

Fort Lockhart Gurudawara

A group of Singhs play Sikh spiritual music. Lucy and Ragi sit in meditation pose. After a few moments, the Sikhs finish playing and Ragi and Lucy open their eyes.

LUCY

Ragi... I don't know how to ask this. The Empire views colored people as less. How do you deal with this attitude? Does it not anger you?

RAGI

Enough to set the Queen's castle a blaze. Enough to shoot every British Officer on the planet.

LUCY

What prevents you?

RAGI

If I indulge in my anger, I only hurt myself. Every living thing emanates a subtle essence. Anger contaminates this essence and a corrupt invisible presence will damage my spiritual progress. And isn't this the goal - to embrace our spiritual potential. To evolve.

LUCY

I want to torch my father's office.

MAJOR RAGI

(laughingly)

What brings this on?

LUCY

The same anger you somehow control.

MAJOR RAGI

(in a serious tone)

You might be a little too white for this.

Lucy gives Ragi a strange look. Ragi breaks his stern look and smiles.

Lucy and Ragi exit the Gurudawara and walk toward the General's office.

MAJOR RAGI

Do you feel better?

LUCY

Much better. What is it about this type of music? I do not understand the words yet I feel good listening to it.

MAJOR RAGI

Vibrations.

LUCY

Mr. Michael Faraday wrote about this. Something to do with human magnetism.

MAJOR RAGI

With the right vibration, anything is possible.

(short pause)

Tell me, what was it that upset you?

LUCY

It is a man's world Ragi and it just is not fair. Men decide what I can and cannot do.

RAGI

What are you not permitted to do?

LUCY

To write the biggest story of the century. Lord Mcleod is missing and my father will not allow me to write the story.

Ragi stops walking. Lucy does too.

RAGI

Lord Mcleod is missing? How long?

LUCY

Several days.

RAGI

I must speak to your father.

LUCY

Will you convince him to do this?

Hughes, dressed in local wear, is waiting for Ragi outside the building to General Andrews' office. Ragi and Lucy approach.

MAJOR RAGI

I will speak with you tomorrow morning. Have a good night Lucy.

LUCY

Okay.

Lucy walks in the opposite direction. Ragi is nearing Hughes.

MAJOR RAGI

Waiting long?

LIEUTENANT HUGHES

No.

They both walk into the building.

The General is drinking tea and reading. The General's secretary knocks and enters. The Major and the Captain enter behind the secretary. Huckslee exits the room.

MAJOR RAGI AND LIEUTENANT HUGHES

(as both salute the General)

General.

GENERAL ANDREWS

Major Ragi. Lieutenant Hughes. What did you discover?

MAJOR RAGI

The Afghan tribes are gathering, soon after the new moon.

LIEUTENANT HUGHES

A spy was stationed a short distance from Lockhart. We chased him off. They too are gathering intel.

MAJOR RAGI

Peshawar is also infested.

GENERAL ANDREWS

What is their intention?

MAJOR RAGI

Domination.

GENERAL ANDREWS

How do they plan to?

MAJOR RAGI

Brute force and cunning. They will attack when we least expect it, and they will attack in the tens-of-thousands.

GENERAL ANDREWS

HUCKSLEE.

The General's secretary rushes into the office.

SECRETARY HUCKSLEE

Yes General.

GENERAL ANDREWS

Please write to General Frankland at Gullistan, and General Fleet at Sarighari. Find out how many men and guns they can spare.

Huckslee exits the office.

GENERAL ANDREWS

Major Ragi. Another concern looms. Lord Stoker Mcleod's expedition is missing. Possibly killed. I need you to investigate. The lieutenant will assist you.

General Andrews hands Major Ragi a letter.

GENERAL ANDREWS

Provided by Lord Mcleod's assistant. All the details of his expedition are there.

Major Ragi skims through the letter.

MAJOR RAGI

What?

Hughes is curious. Ragi gives Hughes the letter to read.

GENERAL ANDREWS

As you know, resources and manpower are limited, and with this possible attack, you have not much to work with.

LIEUTENANT HUGHES

(laughs)

General. I think this is an error.

(POINTING to the word "Devil" on the page)

GENERAL ANDREWS

This is no error. This is the mystery. I understand you work with an Afghan spy living in Peshawar.

LIEUTENANT HUGHES

Yes.

GENERAL ANDREWS

Casually tell him that 20 000 British troops are soon to arrive.

LIEUTENANT HUGHES

I am meeting him tonight.

GENERAL ANDREWS

That is all gentlemen.

Hughes salutes the General and exits. Ragi stays.

MAJOR RAGI

I spoke with Lucy.

GENERAL ANDREWS

(in a stern tone)

Do not encourage her.

MAJOR RAGI

She is a talented writer. Honour will come to the Andrews name.

GENERAL ANDREWS

Her name will not be Andrews much longer. Baron Piar and I are in negotiations. His son will complete his medical studies next year. Lucy will be back in England by that time.

MAJOR RAGI

How does Lucy feel about these negotiations?

GENERAL ANDREWS

I have not discussed this with her. And I suggest you not either.

MAJOR RAGI

This is a mistake. Her future should be decided by her.

GENERAL ANDREWS

This is not the time.

Major Ragi salutes the General.

GENERAL ANDREWS

Good luck Major.

Major Ragi exits. Hughes is waiting outside on his horse.

MAJOR RAGI

What are you waiting for?

LIEUTENANT HUGHES

Where are these soldiers coming from?

MAJOR RAGI

What soldiers?

LIEUTENANT HUGHES

The 20 000.

MAJOR RAGI

No soldiers are coming.

LIEUTENANT HUGHES

Then what is the General on about?

MAJOR RAGI

If the Afghans believe 20 000 troops are arriving soon, they will not so easily commit to an attack.

LIEUTENANT HUGHES

Will it work?

MAJOR RAGI

We will find out together.

They both laugh. Hughes rides off.

Swami Faki's Home

Swami Faki is sitting in a luxurious chair, one of three, and on the roof of his house. The rooftops of Indian homes are typically flat and accessible. The Swami is reading. Charan walks up the stairs with tea and places the tea on the table resting by the Swami. The Swami ignores Charan.

CHARAN

The study is very unorganized. Would you like me to tidy up now or after we return from Lockhart?

Swami sips his tea, but does not look at Charan.

SWAMI FAKI

Now might be best.

Charan nods his head and exits the rooftop. Swami Faki continues to read. Nadira Faki, Swami Faki's daughter, is walking up the staircase as Charan is walking down. Nadira sits on the chair next to the Swami. She is nineteen years of age, slim, beautiful, dark-haired, and light skinned.

NADIRA FAKI

What are you reading?

SWAMI FAKI

Chemistry.

NADIRA FAKI

But you said this morning European books have no worth?

Swami Faki laughs.

SWAMI FAKI

Oh my daughter, chemistry is not a European creation. The understanding of this science comes from India. These Europeans are yet to discover what the ancient masters recorded in this book, 3000 years ago. From this book came the knowledge to heal the Raja of Patialla when he fell from his horse last summer.

NADIRA FAKI

He was unable to move. How did you heal him?

SWAMI FAKI

Gold flakes, mixed in a small amount of water, and sealed in a capsule. 3 times a day for 3 days.

NADIRA FAKI

Hmmm... is that it?

SWAMI FAKI

No. This capsule must be exposed to the appropriate procedure before it can heal.

NADIRA FAKI

What does this procedure do?

SWAMI FAKI

(brief pause)

It infuses the power of the Universe into the capsule.

NADIRA FAKI

Can you teach me?

SWAMI FAKI

Destiny has chosen you not to learn. Perhaps in a future life. For now, pray often. Your fortune might gift a rebirth as a son.

NADIRA FAKI

(with her head down)

Yes.

Nadira gets up and walks to the stair case.

SWAMI FAKI

Where to?

NADIRA FAKI

To my room. Maybe the walls are willing to teach me.

Swami Faki looks at her disappointingly. Nadira makes her way to her room and sits before a desk with a mirror. She grooms her hair. She then gets up and grabs a shawl. She wraps her upper body and covers her head with the shawl. Nadira then walks to the window and climbs out.

Nadira and Hughes

Hughes is standing and leaned up against a tree, a short distance from the Faki home. He examines the night stars. Not too long into it, Nadira enters the scene. The two hug each other and continue to hold each other as if they were apart for many months.

Ragi's Quarter

Ragi and Hughes share a room. The two sleep in their separate beds. The Lieutenant hears a voice and opens his eyes. He hears the voice again. It's coming through the walls. It's Lucy.

LUCY

Ragi.

LIEUTENANT HUGHES

(groggy)

Major.

Lucy is standing facing the door to Ragi's quarters. Ragi opens the door.

MAJOR RAGI

Good morning Lucy. Although, I did not mean you to find me this early.

LUCY

Ragi. Ummm... good morning. How was your sleep? Did, did my father change his mind?

MAJOR RAGI

Lucy. The day is just beginning.

LUCY

I know. I know. Prayer first. But that is why I'm here, now. I want to talk to you before you start your day.

(puts her head down)

I guess I should know better. I am sorry Ragi.

MAJOR RAGI

Since you are up, meet me at the Gurudawara; 30 minutes. We will talk after.

LUCY

Okay.

Ragi shuts the door. Hughes is up and sitting on the edge of his bed.

MAJOR RAGI

She is a good woman. A gem.

(short pause)

You're unmarried.

Lieutenant Hughes snickers.

MAJOR RAGI

You returned to the fort past curfew again.

LIEUTENANT HUGHES

The informant was late.

MAJOR RAGI

Anything?

LIEUTENANT HUGHES

No.

MAJOR RAGI

The Afghans will attack. It is in their nature. We do not have enough men to thwart a surprise assault. Our survival depends on our preparedness Lieutenant. Perhaps you need to find a new spy? One not so... attractive.

With his bath towel over his shoulder, the Major leaves the area. Lieutenant Hughes ponders. Ragi obviously knows that Hughes was with Swami Faki's daughter and not the spy. Hughes is wondering if he should tell the Major, and if so, how. Hughes lied and Ragi doesn't like liars.

William's Room

William is having a nightmare. William wakes in a sweat and screaming. Soon after, Tristan bursts into the room. Tristan surveils the room, looking for the reason William screamed. He sees nothing out of the ordinary. Tristan then concludes the cause.

TRISTAN JACOBS

William. The nightmares. Maybe it is time to see a professional?

WILLIAM MCLEOD

There is nothing they can do.

TRISTAN JACOBS

You are not responsible.

WILLIAM MCLEOD

I am responsible.

TRISTAN JACOBS

William, please, listen to me. It is time to move on.

William stares at Tristan angrily and lashes out.

WILLIAM MCLEOD

You are a hired hand. My father's lacky. Who are you to tell me what to do?

Tristan, with his head up, wet eyed, leaves the room.

As Tristan is standing outside William's room. he drops his head and wipes dry his eyes.

Bad News

Lucy and William exit the Gurudawara.

LUCY

I guess my father did not agree. Why else the wait?

MAJOR RAGI

There will be other opportunities.

The Mcleod Kitchen

The Mcleod estate is simple and situated on beautiful landscape. The estate is surrounded by thick and tall brick walls. The bathing area and lavatory are in a separate building, at the back of the estate. Tristan is in the kitchen and preparing tea. William walks into the kitchen.

WILLIAM MCLEOD

I am sorry Tristan. I lost myself.

Tristan does not respond.

WILLIAM MCLEOD

Tristan. I apologize.

Tristan still doesn't respond.

TRISTAN JACOBS

Sometimes an apology is not enough.

WILLIAM MCLEOD

What can I do?

TRISTAN JACOBS

Sweep that mess by the table.

WILLIAM MCLEOD

What?

TRISTAN JACOBS

Too good to clean?

William grabs the broom and quickly sweeps the mess.

WILLIAM MCLEOD

(in a butler type voice)

Anything else sir?

TRISTAN JACOBS

Yes.

(Tristan sits down)

Two cups please.

William walks to the teapot and pours two cups of tea. He then sets the two cups on the table, before Tristan.

WILLIAM MCLEOD

(lightly and sarcastically)

I typically request one.

Tristan and William laugh. William sits down. Tristan slides him a cup of tea.

WILLIAM MCLEOD

Tristan. Do you know the route my father travelled?

TRISTAN JACOBS

In my journal, there is a map.

Anangh

Servants are preparing for the day. Swami Faki, Grandfather Faki, Anagh Faki, and Nadira Faki sit in the courtyard and enjoy morning tea.

GRANDFATHER FAKI

What did you learn?

Swami Faki remains silent.

GRANDFATHER FAKI

Return to Lockhart. Discover the General's plans.

ANAGH FAKI

What is this about?

SWAMI FAKI

Your grandfather speaks of a myth.

GRANDFATHER FAKI

An opportunity.

ANAGH FAKI

For what?

GRANDFATHER FAKI

To increase our power, your power. A rare beast roams the jungles of Kashmir. We must capture it.

Peshawar Bazaar

William and Tristan walk the Peshawar Bazaar. They enter a supply shop and browse a few items, before examining a bag. The Shopkeeper enters from the back room.

SHOPKEEPER

Hello friends. A beautiful day. That is a good bag. The strongest.

WILLIAM MCLEOD

Do you have one more?

SHOPKEEPER

Hmm... Let me see.

Shopkeeper walks to the back. William looks to Tristan.

WILLIAM MCLEOD

Where can we hire a guide?

TRISTAN JACOBS

I am not sure. Perhaps the Shopkeeper knows. William, we should wait for the General.

William doesn't answer and continues to look forward. The Shopkeeper returns and places the bag on the counter. William pats himself down. William looks at Tristan.

TRISTAN JACOBS

(looks to the Shopkeeper)

How much?

SHOPKEEPER

Five rupees.

Tristan reaches into the inside pocket of his jacket and pulls out his wallet.

TRISTAN JACOBS

(as he pays)

We would like to hire a guide. Someone who knows the Kashmiri jungle.

SHOPKEEPER

I see. Now is not a good time to visit Kashmir. An evil thing is lurking. No guide will travel there.

WILLIAM MCLEOD

Please explain.

SHOPKEEPER

A British team journeyed there. They performed some kind of sacrificial ritual. A demon rose from the earth. This evil devoured them all and is now loss.

WILLIAM MCLEOD

How do you know this?

SHOPKEEPER

There is a survivor.

WILLIAM MCLEOD

Is this his story?

SHOPKEEPER

Yes.

WILLIAM MCLEOD

Did he tell you?

SHOPKEEPER

No. Everyone in Peshawar knows.

WILLIAM MCLEOD

I see. Well, thank you for the bags.

SHOPKEEPER

Be safe my friends.

William and Tristan exit the shop and onto the street.

WILLIAM MCLEOD

The General was adamant he shared everything with me. Why did he not mention the ritual?

TRISTAN JACOBS

William, your father was not that sort of man. Gossip. There was no ritual.

(Tristan points to a Darbar)

Perhaps we should check here.

The two walk into a Darbar (open air cafe). They sit at the nearest table. The waiter arrives.

TRISTAN JACOBS

Two chai please.

WILLIAM MCLEOD

And we search for a guide. Is there anyone here that fits the bill?

WAITER

Possibly.

The waiter leaves. As William and Tristan converse, in the background, the waiter is seen walking to the kitchen and talking to the man who is preparing the tea. The waiter then walks to another man, A guide, far in the back corner.

WILLIAM MCLEOD

How many elephants do I need?

TRISTAN JACOBS

If we can find four, I think we might be good.

WILLIAM MCLEOD

There is no "we" Tristan. I need you here. If I do not return, you will settle my father's affairs.

The Guide approaches the table. He sits.

GUIDE

Where would you like to go?

WILLIAM MCLEOD

(short pause)

The jungle of Kashmir.

The Guide laughs.

WILLIAM MCLEOD

You will earn as much as you do in one year.

GUIDE

What use is gold to a dead man. This is not the time to sightsee in Kashmir.

(brief pause)

An ancient civilization was recently uncovered, Mohenjo-daro. I can take you there. It is older than any place on earth.

WILLIAM MCLEOD

Another time. Kashmir first.

The Guide gets ups.

GUIDE

Another time it is.

The Guide leaves. The Waiter approaches with two cups of chai and sets them on the table.

WAITER

That man is the best Guide in Peshawar. He will take care of you.

WILLIAM MCLEOD

He is afraid.

WAITER

Kashmir? Is this where you wish to go?

WILLIAM MCLEOD

Is there anyone brave enough?

WAITER

You mean, is there anyone foolish enough.

TRISTAN JACOBS

We will pay their year's worth.

A drunken man, Timar, enters the Darbar. The Waiter sees him. Timar sits down at a table.

WAITER

Let me see what I can do.

The waiter walks to the drunken man.

TIMAR

Whiskey please.

WAITER

You still owe from yesterday, and the day before that, and the day before that. Do you have money?

TIMAR

Ahhh... You know I pay. Next week.

WAITER

Listen. I have an idea. Those two

(pointing to William and Tristan)

have a lot of money. They need a Guide. You can take them.

TIMAR

How much money?

WAITER

You will drink every day, for a year.

TIMAR

I like that.

Timar gets up.

WAITER

Wait, let me speak with them. I might be able to negotiate more money.

TIMAR

Good idea.

Timar sits down. The Waiter walks to William and Tristan.

WAITER

He wants more money. Double. Half now.

WILLIAM MCLEOD

Okay.

The Waiter holds out his hand.

WAITER

I will take it to him.

Tristan reaches into his jacket pocket, pulls out his wallet, counts several bills, and cautiously hands the money to the Waiter. The Waiter walks back to Timar's table, and as he is, he cuffs all the bills.

WAITER

Bad news. They did not agree.

TIMAR

Ah. One year is enough. When will they pay?

WAITER

On your return. Shall we meet them.

TIMAR

Lead the way.

The Waiter and Timar walk to Tristan and William's table. Timar steps up.

TIMAR

Timar,

(salutes)

at your service.

WILLIAM MCLEOD

Have a seat? Are you familiar with the Kashmiri jungles.

TIMAR

Kashmir?

WILLIAM MCLEOD

Is there a problem?

TIMAR

Yes.

WILLIAM MCLEOD

There is nothing to fear.

TIMAR

Sure there is. The devil lives there.

(short pause)

She will devour me.

TRISTAN JACOBS

She?

TIMAR

My wife.

William laughs.

WILLIAM MCLEOD

I will protect you Timar.

TIMAR

The entire British Army could not.

(Timar looks at the Whiskey bottle resting on the table next to him)

When do we leave?

TRISTAN JACOBS

Meet us at Edwards Gate tomorrow morning.

TIMAR

Tomorrow then.

Outnumbered and Outgunned

MAJOR RAGI

We do not have enough men for the expedition and to defend Lockhart simultaneously. Any word from the Generals?

GENERAL ANDREWS

Gullistan and Saraghari also seek men and bullets.

MAJOR RAGI

It might be best to wait for reinforcements.

GENERAL ANDREWS

They arrive in two weeks. I need you en route by tomorrow morning.

MAJOR RAGI

Sir, waiting is the ideal.

GENERAL ANDREWS

If this was someone else, I might agree. When word of this reaches Buckingham, they will scrutinize ever step I took from the minute I learned of this. Powerful people need Mcleod alive. Two weeks will cost me my head.

The Major exits the building. The Lieutenant waits outside.

MAJOR RAGI

It looks like you and me again.

LIEUTENANT HUGHES

What about Stoker's son? He will come.

MAJOR RAGI

Do you know where he is?

LIEUTENANT HUGHES

I know where the Mcleod Villa is.

MAJOR RAGI

Ride out there. Recruit the Captain.

LIEUTENANT HUGHES

He's a Captain?

MAJOR RAGI

Yes. A tough one at that.

LIEUTENANT HUGHES

When do we leave for Kashmir?

MAJOR RAGI

In the morning.

The Lieutenant walks away.

MAJOR RAGI

And Lieutenant, we need elephants.

Elephant Market

William and Tristan are standing at the entrance to the Elephant Market. They stare at two sick elephants. Two Elephant Keepers sit in the distance, at a table, playing cards. One of the two sees William and Tristan and he makes his way to them.

ELEPHANT KEEPER

It was something they ate. The healthy were taken this morning. They will not be back for another month.

William looks at Tristan.

WILLIAM MCLEOD

What about horses?

TRISTAN JACOBS

Second best option.

(looks at the Elephant Keeper)

Thank you.

ELEPHANT KEEPER

Good luck.

William and Tristan exit the Elephant Market.

TRISTAN JACOBS

This way William?

Tristan starts to walk in the direction of the Horse Market.

WILLIAM MCLEOD

What about men?

TRISTAN JACOBS

If the Waiter is correct, this might be a problem?

They enter the Horse Market. Tristan sees an old man lying on a cot, under the shade of a tree, but no horses. William and Tristan walk to him.

WILLIAM MCLEOD

Good day sir.

The old man opens his eyes and slowly sits up.

TRISTAN JACOBS

Can we purchase horses here?

OLD MAN

No more. All bought this morning.

TRISTAN JACOBS

All?

OLD MAN

Yes. Two Afghanie businessmen.

WILLIAM MCLEOD

How many?

OLD MAN

729.

WILLIAM MCLEOD

Why did they need all these horses?

OLD MAN

(The old man examines William)

They paid double. I did not ask.

OLD MAN

You are Mcleod's boy. I knew your father. I met him when he first arrived. I sold him my best horse. You have the same presence.

WILLIAM MCLEOD

What type is that?

OLD MAN

A king.

William laughs.

WILLIAM MCLEOD

I am a soldier.

OLD MAN

That changed when your father died.

WILLIAM MCLEOD

He is not dead.

OLD MAN

Is this why you require horses?

WILLIAM MCLEOD

What do you know?

OLD MAN

I know Kashmir. I know the evil that lives there.

The old man shares with William and Tristan the story of Sihindi.

OLD MAN

200 years ago, Abdula Khan, the son of a wealthy Afghan landowner, and his army, set out to spread the true religion. Upon invading Kashmir, Abdula and his army sacked many villages. Village after village fell.

This changed the day he rode into a small village, near the Kashmir jungle. Initially, Abdula faced no resistance and Abdula's men captured and shackled the people. That night, Abdula's men murdered all those who did not convert. In doing so, they killed a witch's husband. During the night, the witch escaped into the jungle. There she summoned a powerful and evil spirit. The next morning the Khan and his men were dead and no villager was near.

WILLIAM MCLEOD

Has anyone attempted to hunt this darkness?

OLD MAN

Yes. Many. All died. You will too.

WILLIAM MCLEOD

(short pause)

Thank you for your time.

William and Tristan leave the Horse Market and walk the street.

TRISTAN JACOBS

No elephants. No horses. A drunk Guide. Should we bother with men?

WILLIAM MCLEOD

Walking is still an option.

TRISTAN JACOBS

Did any of the man's story sink in?

WILLIAM MCLEOD

No. But I am hungry.

Dudley

Alan is alone in the kitchen, sitting on a chair, with a small ball in his hand. It appears as if he's showing the ball to something. Alan then gently tosses the ball and the ball is tossed back. This happens another two times before William and Tristan enter the kitchen.

ALAN STUDWICK

Ah... There you be?

As Alan greets William and Tristan, the ball hit's Alan in the back of the head. Tristan looks in the direction from which the ball came and sees Dudley, the monkey.

TRISTAN JACOBS

Dudley!

Dudley runs to Tristan and hugs him.

TRISTAN JACOBS

Where have you been?

(Tristan exams Dudley)

You were gone for days.

WILLIAM MCLEOD

(looking at Alan)

You made a friend.

ALAN STUDWICK

(sarcastically)

Ha, ha... ha.

William grins.

A knock at the door is heard. Tristan walks to the front door. Lieutenant Hughes has reached the Mcleod Villa. Tristan answers the door.

TRISTAN JACOBS

Hello.

LIEUTENANT HUGHES

My name is Lieutenant Hughes. May I speak with Captain Mcleod.

TRISTAN JACOBS

Please come in.

William is playing with Dudley and the two pass a small ball to each other. Alan is eating. Tristan walks into the kitchen with the Lieutenant.

WILLIAM MCLEOD

Where did you find Dudley?

TRISTAN JACOBS

He was a gift to your father, from the Maharaja of Patiala. A Lieutenant Hughes is here to see you.

William looks away from Dudley. The Lieutenant salutes William and William salutes back. Dudley throws the ball at William and the ball hits William on the side of the face.

LIEUTENANT HUGHES

Major Ragi wishes I speak with you. The Major is leading the rescue mission.

WILLIAM MCLEOD

Let me guess, it is taking longer to organize than anticipated.

LIEUTENANT HUGHES

Not quite. We leave in the morning. However, we lack men and resources. A potential tribal incursion prevents the forts from helping, until reinforcements arrive, in two weeks.

WILLIAM MCLEOD

How many men have you mustered? How many mercenaries?

LIEUTENANT HUGHES

Myself and the Major. The local guns are not interested.

WILLIAM MCLEOD

(pause)

You have two more Lieutenant. From where do we leave?

LIEUTENANT HUGHES

Fort Lockhart. The Main gate – Edwards Gate. Who is the other?

WILLIAM MCLEOD

Mr. Studwick.

Alan stops eating, looks at William wide-eyed, and then shakes his head.

LIEUTENANT HUGHES

Alright. Thank you. Elephants are next on my list. I must go.

WILLIAM MCLEOD

There are no elephants.

TRISTAN JACOBS

Nor any horses.

The Drive

The Swami, Anagh, and Charan ride to Lockhart. Charan drives.

ANAGH JUKI

Father, what creature can possibly do what you and Grandfather suggest?

SWAMI FAKI

Your Grandfather is old. He is imagining things.

ANAGH FAKI

What is he imagining?

SWAMI FAKI

A creature able to empower our family as living gods.

ANAGH FAKI

How?

SWAMI FAKI

Your Grandfather is speaking nonsense.

ANAGH FAKI

Then why are we travelling to Lockhart?

SWAMI FAKI

Just in case. Besides, you have nothing better to do.

ANAGH FAKI

Sleep.

Swami Faki laughs.

Rookie

General Andrews and Major Ragi are talking and examining an artifact. The General is a part-time archeologist.

GENERAL ANDREWS

This here I uncovered in the central Punjab area. We are yet to decipher the language.

MAJOR RAGI

Mohenjo-daro. The Indus Civilization.

GENERAL ANDREWS

Yes. Larger than ancient Egypt and Sumer combined.

There's a knock at the door.

GENERAL ANDREWS

Come.

Huckslee enters.

HUCKSLEE

The Swami and his son are here to see you.

GENERAL ANDREWS

Let them in.

Huckslee exits. The General hands Ragi the artifact.

GENERAL ANDREWS

What do you think the image represents?

Huckslee is back, accompanied by the Swami and Anagh. Ragi is examining the artifact.

GENERAL ANDREWS

Swami. What brings you to Lockhart?

SWAMI FAKI

The people are still very concerned General. I am here to learn what you plan to do.

GENERAL ANDREWS

Give us time to investigate. The Major leaves in the morning.

SWAMI FAKI

Major, my son will accompany you.

MAJOR RAGI

(as he hands the artifact to the General)

A man practicing Siddhasana, a type of yoga.

GENERAL ANDREWS

Yes. Of course.

Ragi looks to Anagh.

MAJOR RAGI

Do you have any military training son?

ANAGH FAKI

No.

MAJOR RAGI

Have you hunted?

ANAGH FAKI

No.

MAJOR RAGI

Can you fire a rifle?

ANAGH FAKI

(puts his head down)

No.

MAJOR RAGI

Then I am sorry.

SWAMI FAKI

He is strong and intelligent. He will be an asset.

MAJOR RAGI

Or a liability. I do not know what I will encounter. I require experience.

SWAMI FAKI

Yes, yes. On your return, please share your findings. Good day Major. Good day General.

Huckslee stands at the door and opens the door to allow the Swami and Anagh to exit. As the Swami exits the office, Lucy, in a rush, enters from the main door.

SWAMI FAKI

Miss Andrews.

Lucy smiles and rushes past the Swami and Anagh.

LUCY

Father, I am leaving to stay with Aunt Becky.

GENERAL ANDREWS

Delhi? Your aunt lives in Delhi.

LUCY

Yes.

GENERAL ANDREWS

Why?

LUCY

Research.

Lucy quickly exits the office. The General, Ragi, and Huckslee don't know what to make of this.

Backdoor

The Swami, Anagh, and Charan travel in the Swami's car back to the Faki home.

SWAMI FAKI

(leans forward to the driver)

Make your way to the Mcleod Villa.

ANAGH FAKI

Why are we heading there?

Charan takes a left.

SWAMI FAKI

We need you to join the expedition.

ANAGH FAKI

But the Major said no.

SWAMI FAKI

He is only a Major. We are on our way to persuade the son of the wealthiest man. If we are lucky, he will be with the Major tomorrow.

The Front Yard

William and Tristan stand in the front yard of the Mcleod Villa.

WILLIAM MCLEOD

We need more men.

TRISTAN JACOBS

Perhaps the weapons inventor.

WILLIAM MCLEOD

What weapons inventor?

TRISTAN JACOBS

Your father commissioned a weapons master to build his designs.

The Swami's vehicle pulls up. The Swami and Anagh quickly get out and walk toward William and Tristan.

TRISTAN JACOBS

Good day Swami.

SWAMI FAKI

To you as well.

Swami Faki turns his attention to William.

SWAMI FAKI

Mr. Mcleod, it is nice to see you again. I hope you are well.

WILLIAM MCLEOD

Yes. Swami...?

SWAMI FAKI

Faki.

WILLIAM MCLEOD

How may I help you Mr. Faki.

Tristan is leaving.

TRISTAN JACOBS

William, I will be back soon.

WILLIAM MCLEOD

Where to?

TRISTAN JACOBS

To recruit.

Leaving a Lover

Nadira is shopping for vegetables. Lieutenant Hughes rides through the Bazaar. He sees Nadira shopping. Nadira sees him. Nadira purchases the onions and walks off. Hughes follows. Nadira reaches a secluded area.

LIEUTENANT HUGHES
I'm happy to see you.
(short pause)
I have something to tell you. I'm leaving for a few weeks.

The Lieutenant stands facing Lucy, with one hand on the building.

NADIRA FAKI
Where to?

LIEUTENANT HUGHES
To find a missing person. Kashmir.

NADIRA FAKI
No. Stay.

LIEUTENANT HUGHES
What is it?

NADIRA FAKI

I know what is out there. I overheard my grandfather and father talk.

LIEUTENANT HUGHES

What do you know?

NADIRA FAKI

There is a creature with immense power. It devours everything living. My grandfather desires to catch it and take its power. But no one can trap it. One look into its eyes and a man is unable to move. That is when it attacks.

LIEUTENANT HUGHES

Forget all that. Fairytales. Tell me, have you told your father about me?

NADIRA FAKI

No. He wishes I marry a Brahmin or a wealthy man. I do not know what he will do if I tell him about you. He might kill me.

The Lieutenant doesn't know what to say. The Lieutenant embraces Nadira.

Delhi

As Lieutenant Hughes rides into Lockhart and to the stable, he sees Lucy with several suitcases and entering a carriage. The carriage leaves the fort and toward the direction of Peshawar. Lieutenant Hughes secures his horse and makes his way to his quarters.

Ragi sits on his bed and reads. Hughes enters.

LIEUTENANT HUGHES

I saw Lucy packed and leaving.

MAJOR RAGI

She left for Delhi.

LIEUTENANT HUGHES

Why?

Ragi puts his book down.

MAJOR RAGI

I do not know.

LIEUTENANT HUGHES

William and his friend Alan will join us.

MAJOR RAGI

The elephants?

LIEUTENANT HUGHES

All are taken.

MAJOR RAGI

Did you check for horses?

LIEUTENANT HUGHES

No horses.

MAJOR RAGI

The fort can only spare two horses and we need them to carry our supplies. I suppose we walk.

LIEUTENANT HUGHES

Listen. Ragi. I need to tell you something.

MAJOR RAGI

What is it?

LIEUTENANT HUGHES

Nadira Faki.

MAJOR RAGI

I know. What are your intentions?

LIEUTENANT HUGHES

How do you know?

MAJOR RAGI

Your spy came to see me. I worried. I went looking for you and I found you.

LIEUTENANT HUGHES

I am sorry Ragi.

MAJOR RAGI

The spy had nothing important to tell, and I delivered the misinformation.

(short pause)

What do you plan to do with Miss Faki?

LIEUTENANT HUGHES

Marry her. But...

MAJOR RAGI

Her father. I understand.

LIEUTENANT HUGHES

What should I do?

MAJOR RAGI

Forget her, unless you are willing to fight for her. And a fight it will be. Her father will try to kill you.

LIEUTENANT HUGHES

Will you help me?

MAJOR RAGI

From a distance. This is your mess Lieutenant.

LIEUTENANT HUGHES

I cannot live without her. I love her.

Ragi laughs.

LIEUTENANT HUGHES

Why are you laughing.

MAJOR RAGI

Love. It is a funny thing.

A Mission Within

Grandfather Faki is sitting on a chair, drinking tea. Anagh approaches and sits down.

GRANDFATHER FAKI

Are you prepared for tomorrow?

ANAGH FAKI

Yes. I've gathered what I need.

GRANDFATHER FAKI

Watch everything. Learn everything.

ANAGH FAKI

Yes.

GRANDFATHER FAKI

One more task. Come closer.

Anagh leans in and Grandfather Faki whispers in Anagh's ear. Anagh's eyes widen. Anagh is still. Anagh is speechless.

The Journey Begins

William, Alan, and Anagh are walking to Fort Lockhart. They each carry their own supplies. A short distance behind them, and running to catch-up, is Timar.

ALAN STUDWICK

William, I like you, but no horses, no elephants, and these huge bags. I do not know if our friendship can survive this. Dudley would never do this to me.

William laughs.

ALAN STUDWICK

Tristan's horse?

WILLIAM MCLEOD

I forgot Tristan had a horse.

(laughs)

William hears Timar approaching from behind. William turns his head.

WILLIAM MCLEOD

Timar. Good morning. Excellent timing.

TIMAR

Good morning sir.

WILLIAM MCLEOD

Alan, Anagh, this is Timar, our Guide.

As they walk, Alan reaches over and shakes Timar's hand. Anagh too shakes Timar's hand. The four reach Fort Lockhart and Ragi and Hughes, outside the main gate, are loading two horses with supplies.

MAJOR RAGI

Captain Mcleod.

WILLIAM MCLEOD

Major. This is Alan Studwick, Timar, and...

MAJOR RAGI

Anagh. Where there is a will there is a way. Is that not how the saying goes.

(Ragi looks to all)

The horses will carry the bags. Let's move.

WILLIAM MCLEOD

One more is coming.

Tristan and Aree enter the scene. Aree pulls a donkey loaded with cargo behind her.

TRISTAN JACOBS

William, Major Ragi, this is Aree.

Ragi examines Aree. He's not impressed. Aree senses this. She reaches into her satchel and pulls out a large, single-shot handgun. She throws the gun at Ragi. Ragi catches it. Aree then pulls out a bullet the size of a ping-pong ball and throws it at Ragi. Ragi catches this too.

MAJOR RAGI

Where is this from?

AREE

I built it.

MAJOR RAGI

What can it do?

AREE

It will blow the target into bits. The bullet explodes two seconds after impact.

Ragi hands the weapon to William. William examines it.

MAJOR RAGI

What else do you have?

Aree reaches into her satchel, pulls out another handgun, but smaller, loads it, and hands it to Ragi.

AREE

It fires twelve bullets before a reload.

Ragi takes aim at a massive log resting forty feet away.

AREE

If you hold the trigger, the bullets fire one after another.

Ragi opens fire. He squeezes out twelve shots. Ragi is impressed. The log is in pieces. Aree again reaches into her satchel. She pulls out a bag of bullets and throws it at Ragi. William is seen in the background loading the larger handgun. Ragi catches the bag of bullets.

AREE

Five more reloads in there.

William aims the gun at a tree and fires. The tree explodes. All are surprised.

MAJOR RAGI

What other surprises do you have?

AREE

Everything on Theo.

MAJOR RAGI

Theo?

Aree points to the donkey. Ragi lightly laughs.

MAJOR RAGI

Show me on the way. We have two-and-a-half days before we get there.

(addresses the group)

Alright, let's get going.

The expedition team prepare to leave.

ALAN STUDWICK

Tristan, your horse?

TRISTAN JACOBS

I walked.

ALAN STUDWICK

I guess I will too.

William laughs.

Sihindi's Cave

Sihindi is resting. She lay her head on something soft and furry. A low purring sound is heard. A soft and white light radiates from where Sihindi's head lay. As Sihindi naps, the wrinkles on her face smoothen, her grey hairs reverse back to black, and her muscles tighten. After a few moments, Sihindi wakes. She appears youthful. She walks over to a bowl of water and washes her face. After which, Sihindi walks outside, to a tree, and sits under it, in meditation pose.

Sikh Rebel Camp

Jang Singh and Rattan Singh drink tea and chat.

RATTAN SINGH

When?

JANG SINGH

Tonight.

RATTAN SINGH

How many?

JANG SINGH

Three.

RATTAN SINGH

Will this be enough?

JANG SINGH

Yes.

Three-Days

The General walks the fort walls and inspects the cannons. Captain Fleck walks beside the General.

GENERAL ANDREWS

All reports suggest that a little over 15 000 Waziristanis will swarm.

CAPTAIN FLECK

I was told 10 000. Are we prepared? I will procure more horses and supplies.

GENERAL ANDREWS

We have enough supplies and all the horses were purchased by the Waziristanis. Peshawar is riddled with them.

CAPTAIN FLECK

What do we do?

GENERAL ANDREWS

They prepared for a three-day campaign. We hold them back for three days.

CAPTAIN FLECK

Standing for one day will be a challenge.

GENERAL ANDREWS

Have faith Captain. Greater miracles have occurred on this soil.

Shortly after, the nurse rushes to the courtyard. She spots General Andrews and makes her way to him.

Afghan Invader Camp

An Afghanie soldier runs through the camp, with a letter, and to Ghazi Mirzali Khan Wazir, leader of the Waziristanis. The Waziristanis are Afghanie rebels who still fight the British. The Wazir stands outside, with two Generals: Mustaf and Raheed. They all circle a table with a map of the forts (Lockhart, Saranghari, and Gullistan) and the surrounding areas, with pieces placed on the map signifying the Afghanie attack plan. The Afghanie soldier reaches the Wazir, aka, Faqir Ipi, and hands him the letter. The Wazir reads the letter.

GHAZI MIRZALI KHAN WAZIR

Lockhart is preparing.

Mustaf steps up to the table and reconfigures the pieces to change the battle plan.

MUSTAF

Perhaps we attack only North and South. Assaulting all sides might thin our strength?

GHAZI MIRZALI KHAN WAZIR

Raheed, do you agree?

Raheed is silent.

GHAZI MIRZALI KHAN WAZIR

We hit them from all sides. We have the manpower for it. 100 000 men stand with us.

Outside Sihindi's Cave

Sihindi practices a Rajput martial art style, while a purring and light roar is heard.

SIHINDI

What is it? Hungry?

A light roar is heard.

SIHINDI

You do not need me.

A light roar is heard, slightly different than the previous.

SIHINDI

Ah... Big baby.

Sihindi stops her practice and walks toward her garden. "Something big" follows her.

SIHINDI

You know, you have an entire jungle to choose from.

Sihindi reaches her garden and it is immense. She has all sorts of vegetables and fruits.

Broken Record

The nurse and General Andrews stand by the wounded soldier.

GENERAL ANDREWS

Tell me what you saw?

The wounded soldier is speechless.

GENERAL ANDREWS

We sent a rescue team.

WOUNDED SOLDIER

(short pause)

They will die.

On the way to Kashmir

The expedition team treks through the jungle. They reach an opening.

MAJOR RAGI

Timar, what do you think?

TIMAR

Yes. This is good.

The expedition team stops and sets up camp for the night.

ALAN STUDWICK

It's been one day William and I am ready for my grave.

WILLIAM MCLEOD

The exercise will do you good.

ALAN STUDWICK

No... no it will not. Not at all.

Aree is setting up her tent. The tent is a pop-up type tent. Major Ragi takes notice.

MAJOR RAGI

That was quick. Did you make this too?

AREE

Yes.

MAJOR RAGI

Genius.

Major Ragi examines the tent.

MAJOR RAGI

Can you make me one?

AREE

Hmmm... You can have this when we return.

Major Ragi, still examining the tent, smiles.

On Route to Fort Lockhart

The Singhs are moving through the jungle.

SEVA SINGH

Why are we fighting the British if they plan to return our land? They wait for Dulip to mature. How will we be remembered?

RATTAN SINGH

What makes you think promises will be kept? They desire we not regain our power. Why would they? They fear us.

SEVA SINGH

Why? We do not invade, we do not loot.

RATTAN SINGH

Yes, but they do, and the Khalsa's duty is to destroy those who do. Besides, look how much their strength has grown since taking Punjab. The British will not give back this pot of gold.

SEVA SINGH

Why treat Dulip with such respect?

RATTAN SINGH

He is a pawn. They took him to England and raise him as Christian European Royalty. Once he is prepared, they will seat him as ruler of the Sikhs, but there will be nothing Sikh about him.

SEVA SINGH

Why do all that?

RATTAN SINGH

Seva, brother, the British are cunning, more than any other. They realize we will not accept foreign rule, so they brainwash the last son of Ranjit as their puppet, hoping that we will accept the puppet as King, while they pull the puppet's string.

JANG SINGH

Quite time boys. We near.

The Singhs reach the outskirts of Fort Lockhart.

RATTAN SINGH

What's the plan?

JANG SINGH

We scale the wall, sneak past the soldiers, and open the cell door.

RATTAN SINGH

(sarcastically)

Yes, simple. Then we build a boat and sail to the moon.

JANG SINGH

Watch the guards. We must time this right.

Two British soldiers walk back and forth, on the fort wall. Jang examines their movement and identifies a pattern through which the rebels can make their way in.

JANG SINGH

Alright. On my word. Rattan, follow me. Seva, stay here. Have your rifle ready.

RATTAN SINGH

Do you know your way about?

JANG SINGH

Yes, I was stationed here.

Seva and Rattan, perplexed, look at each other.

RATTAN SINGH

What?

JANG SINGH

(slight smirk)

I once wore the red.

Jang suddenly moves toward the wall. Rattan follows. At the wall, Jang signals Rattan to stay still, as the soldiers are coming back. As the soldiers cross, Jang throws up a lasso and it catches a top piece of the wall. Jang scales the wall and waits near the top, on the outside of the wall, for the soldiers to again cross. He quickly climbs over.

As soon as Jang climbs over, Rattan does the same. The two then maneuver toward the Detention Center.

While passing the building housing the General's office, Jang and Rattan overhear two British soldiers talking, from the adjacent side of the building.

BRITISH SOLDIER 2

The devil?

Jang and Rattan lean against the building to listen.

BRITISH SOLIDER 3

Kashmir is a mysterious place, and those people in the jungles practice witchery. Supposedly, it devoured the entire expedition.

BRITISH SOLDIER 2

Nonsense.

BRITISH SOLDIER 3

Tell that to the guy laying in the infirmary.

BRITISH SOLDIER 2

Whatever it is, Major Ragi will fix it.

Jang signals Rattan to follow him. Jang moves in the opposite direction from the soldiers, and around the other side of the building.

RATTAN SINGH

What were they speaking of?

JANG SINGH

Something that should not exist.

RATTAN SINGH

(confused)

What?

JANG SINGH

Later. We are here.

The two reach the Detention Center and quickly subdue the guard standing inside. They confiscate the keys and free their comrade. Manh Singh salutes the two with both hands together and a slight bow.

MANH SINGH

Waheguru Ji Ke Khalsa, Waheguru Ki Ka Fateh. (God's Khalsa. God's Victory).

Rattan hands Manh a rifle and then picks up the British soldier's rifle. The three exit the center and with lightning speed, they reach the fort wall, from which Jang and Rattan entered. They move up the stairs leading to the top of the wall. Jang takes the lead and encounters a British soldier. Jang quickly eliminates him. They reach the lasso. Suddenly, the alarm bell rings.

One by one, the three scale down the wall. Shots are fired as they run toward Seva. Seva fires back. The three reach Seva, and as they do, they quickly turn and fire toward the fort. After a short moment, the four retreat.

JANG SINGH

Rattan, Seva, Manh. Tomorrow morning we leave for Kashmir.

RATTAN SINGH

Why?

JANG SINGH

To learn if the stories are true?

RATTAN SINGH

What stories?

Camp

The team has settled into their camp. Ragi and William Gatka close to the campfire. Gatka is a form of combat. Anagh sits with Aree and both watch Ragi and William spar. As he spars, Ragi senses something.

WILLIAM MCLEOD

What is it?

MAJOR RAGI

We are watched?

WILLIAM MCLEOD

By who?

MAJOR RAGI

Not sure. Perhaps a predator.

WILLIAM MCLEOD

What?

MAJOR RAGI

Man-eating tigers. This area is known for them.

Anagh watches Hughes intently.

ANAGH FUKI

Do you believe in God?

AREE

Yes, of course. Why do you ask?

ANAGH FUKI

Sometimes I wonder what makes God happy, what makes God angry, what pleases God, what does not.

AREE

What does your Father say?

Anagh's attention is no longer on Hughes and he appears confused.

ANAGH FUKI

He does not understand.

AREE

Ow. Ummm... okay, well, God is not pleased with those who hurt others.

ANAGH FUKI

What if an enemy?

AREE

Who's enemy? Gods?

ANAGH FUKI

Have you killed anyone?

AREE

No. Have you?

ANAGH FUKI

No.

AREE

Could you?

Anagh looks at Hughes.

Tigers

As the expedition team sleep, two vicious man-eating tigers invade the camp. One tiger takes Anagh by the leg and drags him away. Anagh screams. The camp awakens. Mayhem ensues. Ragi pursues Anagh. The second tiger attacks William and pins William to the ground. Alan fires his rifle and hits the second tiger. It's a flesh wound and the tiger turns and pursues Alan.

An individual who followed the expedition, and who slept high in a tree, spots the tiger chasing Alan. The mysterious individual takes aim with a rifle and shots the tiger down.

Ragi reaches Anagh and attempts to fire his rifle. The rifle malfunctions. Ragi draws his sword and lets out an intimidating roar. The tiger turns and rushes Ragi. With one swing of the sword, Ragi kills the tiger.

William reaches Alan and spots the mysterious individual climbing down from a tree. The mysterious character jumps on a horse and rides away.

On Route to Stoker's Camp

It is early morning and the expedition team moves through the jungle.

MAJOR RAGI

Anagh, how is the wound?

ANAGH FAKI

Minor.

MAJOR RAGI

Alan, you?

ALAN STUDWICK

No holes here. Thank you William.

WILLIAM MCLEOD

It was not my bullet.

ALAN STUDWICK

Who do I owe?

WILLIAM MCLEOD

I do not know.

Major Ragi is processing what he hears.

Sikh Rebels on the Move

The Rebels are on horseback.

JANG SINGH

I too once believed what Seva ponders.

RATTAN SINGH

What happened?

JANG SINGH

The British have no intention of returning our land. They are here for one reason, to increase their power. The sooner Punjab realizes this the better.

(short pause)

We need to move quicker.

MANH SINGH

How do you know where to go?

JANG SINGH

My grandfather told me of this place. I know a shortcut.

Failure

GENERAL ANDREWS

Casualties?

CAPTAIN FLECK

No. Wounded only. Our soldiers are tough.

GENERAL ANDREWS

Not tough enough, apparently. He escaped.

General Andrews briefly stares at Fleck.

GENERAL ANDREWS

Can you track them?

CAPTAIN FLECK

No.

Trouble

The expedition team is making progress.

AREE

You know, the folk talk about you. They say you are the ideal man - strong, moral, wise, loyal. Why are you not married?

Ragi laughs.

MAJOR RAGI

I did not realize we knew each other so well.

AREE

Seriously.

MAJOR RAGI

Love is something that missed me.

AREE

Why?

MAJOR RAGI

That is a question for the Heavens.

Timar sees something.

TIMAR

Over there?

The team see Afghan soldiers. The Afghan army is massive.

AREE

There are so many.

LIEUTENANT HUGHES

Ragi, what do we do?

MAJOR RAGI

Lockhart will not survive.

LIEUTENANT HUGHES

I guess the 20 000 soldier trick did not work.

Ragi lightly laughs.

MAJOR RAGI

Perhaps 200 000 might have worked. Quickly, we must hide.

A bullet zooms by William.

WILLIAM MCLEOD

It's too late.

The expedition team quickly move.

The shot came from the center of the Afghan entourage. The Afghanies stop. An Afghanie horseman, from the center, rides to the front and informs Ghazi Mirzali Khan Wazir.

AFGHANIE HORSEMAN

The British.

GHAZI MIRZALI KHAN WAZIR

How many?

AFGHANIE HORSEMAN

I do not know.

GHAZI MIRZALI KHAN WAZIR

Mustaf, destroy them.

Mustaf pursues the team with 1000 foot soldiers.

The expedition team quickly move through the jungle. The Afghans pursue. The expedition team cross a river. A supply horse runs off. The expedition team continue moving through the jungle and eventually reach a mountainside. There is nowhere left to run.

LIEUTENANT HUGHES

Nowhere.

The Afghans fire. The team takes a defensive position behind big boulders and fire back.

MAJOR RAGI

(as he fires his rifle)

Now is the time.

Aree unstraps the cargo from the donkey. She pulls out a grenade launcher type weapon and the weapon's ammo. Hughes and Studwick are the closest to her and she rushes to them. She has their attention.

AREE

Okay, watch me and learn.

Aree loads the weapon and fires. Multiple Afghanie soldiers are taken down. Hughes and Studwick are in awe. She hands the weapon to Hughes and then reaches for another grenade launcher style weapon. This one she gives to Alan. Aree rushes back to the cargo and pulls out a large contraption that fires a dozen arrows simultaneously. Each arrow has a bomb tip. She sets up the machine.

AREE

(loudly)

Anagh. Timar.

Anagh and Timar rush to her. She demonstrates the use of the machine.

AREE

Look. First we load the arrows in here. Then we aim and pull here. Now we light the arrow heads.

Aree pulls the trigger. The arrows cause immense damage to the Afghan forces.

AREE

Timar will aim and pull. Anagh you load and light.

Ragi and William use the weapons Aree gave them earlier.

RAGI

Aree, this is not reaching them.

WILLIAM MCLEOD

They stand too far away.

Aree rushes to the cargo, finds three modified rifles, and throws one at Ragi and one at William. Aree holds the third.

AREE

For distance.

Aree fires her modified rifle and hits a target twice the distance a normal rifle is capable of reaching. Ragi and William fire their rifles.

Pinned

The night has set.

WILLIAM MCLEOD

It is too dark.

MAJOR RAGI

Keep firing. Assume they move in.

TIMAR

I have no more arrows.

MAJOR RAGI

Pick up a rifle and fire.

Aree moves to the cargo and pulls out a grenade launcher type weapon. Aree loads it and fires into the sky, over the enemy. A few seconds later, an explosion is heard and the sky lights up. The enemy is revealed and they are close. Moreover, an Afghan soldier managed to flank the team and now moves to shoot the team members in the back. Just as the soldier is about to fire, he is shot from the side. The shot came from high up in a tree. It's the mysterious individual who's been following the team. The fighting continues, and after a brief push back, the Afghans again close in. The team is close to extermination.

TIMAR

Too many. Too close.

MAJOR RAGI

We fight until they die or we die. Waheguru Ji Ka Khalsa, Waheguru Ji Ka Fateh.

Then suddenly, the Afghans start to fall. Mustaf falls. No one knows who is shooting them down. The Afghans panic. The "mysterious helpers" move from one side to the other side quickly, firing from all sides. The Afghans, confused, retreat.

WILLIAM MCLEOD

(yells out)

Who are you?

The "mysterious helpers" hide behind trees.

JANG SINGH

You can come out.

MAJOR RAGI

(yells out)

Who are you?

JANG SINGH

By virtue of a common enemy, for now, your friend.

MAJOR RAGI

(looks at the team)

It is safe.

ALAN STUDWICK

Who are they?

MAJOR RAGI

Rebel Sikhs.

ALAN STUDWICK

What? Can we trust them?

MAJOR RAGI

If they say they are a friend, then they are a friend.

Mountainside Camp

The team and the rebels sit around a fire. The camp is set where the expedition team held out against the Afghanies.

MAJOR RAGI

How long has it been?

JANG SINGH

Not long enough.

MAJOR RAGI

What are you doing here?

JANG SINGH

Curiosity.

WILLIAM MCLEOD

How do you two know each other?

JANG SINGH

Ragi was my Captain.

(short pause)

But enough about that. Why are the Afghanies here?

MAJOR RAGI

They move toward Lockhart.

JANG SINGH

Why are you here?

MAJOR RAGI

(short pause)

Searching for answers. An expedition team is lost.

WILLIAM MCLEOD

My father is lost.

MANH SINGH

Jang, this is the man, from the train. He captured me.

JANG SINGH

He also destroyed our ammunition. What would you like to do?

Manh stares at William. William returns the look, as he reaches for his pistol.

WILLIAM MCLEOD

Here, a gift.

(as he gives the pistol to Manh)

Manh Singh examines the pistol.

MANH SINGH

This is a nice piece.

WILLIAM MCLEOD

Are we square?

Manh Singh hands the pistol back to William.

MANH SINGH

Keep it. It was a fair fight, and the ammunition, well, it was yours to begin with.

All the Sikh rebels laugh. All others follows suit.

MAJOR RAGI

Jang, help us.

JANG SINGH

With what?

MAJOR RAGI

We do not know what to expect. The more hands holding rifles the better.

There is a moment of silence. Seva desires to help the British. Jang ponders his response.

JANG SINGH

We will accompany you.

RATTAN SINGH

Jang!

JANG SINGH

We do not betray the cause. This is temporary.

Ragi looks at the rebels.

MAJOR RAGI

Thank you.

JANG SINGH

Up in the tree, who is that?

Mystery Solved

It is past midnight, and while everyone sleeps, Jang, Ragi, William, and Alan investigate who is in the tree.

WILLIAM MCLEOD

(as William climbs the tree)

There should be a horse somewhere here.

ALAN STUDWICK

Got it.

Alan looks about for the horse and exits the scene. William spots the mysterious individual's weapons and throws them to Ragi. The mysterious individual wakes and hits William in the chin. The individual's face is covered. William loses balance and falls a few feet before he catches a sturdy branch. William hangs from the tree with both hands. The mysterious individual climbs down the other side of the tree. Ragi and Jang have their rifles pointed at the individual.

THE MYSTERIOUS INDIVIDUAL

Ragi!

RAGI

Lucy. What!

Lucy removes her face covering. Ragi laughs. William jumps to the ground.

RAGI

You cease not to amaze. I would like to introduce you all to Lucy Andrews. General Andrews daughter.

William catches Lucy's attention.

WILLIAM MCLEOD

It is a pleasure to meet you.

(as William rubs his chin)

LUCY

That will teach you to sneak up on a lady.

Everyone laughs. Alan walks up with Lucy's horse.

Afghans on the Move

The Afghanie forces move through the jungle.

RAHEED

Mustaf has not returned. Something is not right.

GHAZI MIRZALI KHAN WAZIR

We march on. If he lives, he will join us.

The Afghan forces appear powerful and dominating.

Early Morning Nightmare

William is having a nightmare. Ragi witnesses William's nightmarish state. William wakes in a sweat.

WILLIAM MCLEOD

(whisper)

Tommy?!

William looks to see if anyone saw him. He thinks no one did. William is the last to wake and all others are slowly preparing to move out.

Aree walks to Lucy and sits beside her. Lucy is writing in her notebook. Anagh stands close by and prepares the supply horse to ride back to Lockhart.

AREE

Hi. Aree.

(as she extends her hand)

LUCY

(as she shakes Aree's hand)

Hi. I am...

AREE

Lucy. I know. Were you not afraid?

LUCY

Of?

AREE

Riding and sleeping in the jungle, alone.

LUCY

Ummm. Not really. I knew Ragi was close by.

AREE

Still. You are amazing.

LUCY

Then you must be too.

AREE

What!

LUCY

You too are out here.

Lucy and Aree smile at each other. Anagh overheard the conversation and also smiles. Hughes and Ragi observe Anagh from the opposite end of the camp.

LIEUTENANT HUGHES

Perhaps send Lucy back to warn Lockhart.

Ragi lightly laughs.

RAGI

Try suggesting that to her.

Timar walks over to Ragi and Hughes.

TIMAR

If nothing obstructs us, we will be there this afternoon.

Anagh is ready to leave. He is happy.

AREE

Anagh, are you not disappointed? You came so far to only turn back.

ANAGH FUKI

(as he hops on the horse)

This is a good day. God is good.

William walks over to Lucy and Aree with two cups of tea. Aree gives Lucy a look and leaves the two be.

WILLIAM MCLEOD

Good morning.

LUCY

Morning.

WILLIAM MCLEOD

(offers tea to Lucy)

You might like this?

LUCY

Oh. Tea. Yes, please.

Lucy accepts the tea from William.

LUCY

Thank you.

(as she is about to sip)

This is tea, right?

WILLIAM MCLEOD

(laughingly)

What else would it be?

LUCY

Poison. I did smuck you good.

Lucy smiles then sips her tea. William laughs and then gestures to Lucy's notebook.

WILLIAM MCLEOD

What are you writing on?

LUCY

This. This journey.

WILLIAM MCLEOD

Did you include your stay in the trees?

LUCY

(sarcastically)

Yes, alongside your fall.

William laughs.

WILLIAM MCLEOD

Who taught you how to hit?

LUCY

Ragi.

As Lucy and William chat, Alan interrupts.

ALAN STUDWICK

We are ready.

WILLIAM MCLEOD

(as he looks at Lucy)

Shall we.

The River

The jungle is still. A person is vaguely seen stumbling through. This person moves through the foliage and toward a river. This individual reaches the river. It's Merritt. He's in bad shape. Merritt proceeds to fill a leather sack with water. As he does, he hears the same roar he heard before his team was attacked. He moves toward the roar to investigate.

Sihindi's Nightmare

Sihindi is having a nightmare. She remembers the day Abdula Khan invaded her village. Images of the invaders battling her lover flood her mind. He wore a dark blue cloth around his waist and fought like a mythical hero. He was outnumbered. Sihindi watched through the window of her home. Sihindi was unable to help, as her parents restrained her. After an honourable fight, Sihindi's lover was killed.

That night Sihindi, with a look of rage and sadness, snuck out from her home and toward the jungle. There she meditated and chanted. Soon after, the goddess Durga appeared. Durga is the Hindu goddess of war and protection.

GODDESS DURGA

I hear you.

Sihindi opens her eyes and sees Durga. As she does, Durga disappears. Soon after, a massive roar is heard.

Sihindi wakes. Tears run down her face. She rises and walks to a box. She pulls out the dark blue cloth her lover wore as he battled. Sihindi ties it about her waist and exits the cave.

Destination

From a clearing, the team see the remains of Stoker's camp. They have reached their destination.

MAJOR RAGI

This is it.

LIEUTENANT HUGHES

What happened?

William runs toward Stoker's camp.

MAJOR RAGI

Wait!

William ignores Ragi. Ragi looks to the team.

MAJOR RAGI

Keep you rifles, unload the rest, and follow me.

The team unloads their gear.

MAJOR RAGI

(as he walks toward camp)

Aree, stay behind. Watch our gear.

Ragi walks toward William. The team lags behind. The camp is burnt to the ground, exempt for a few things and many dozen crates of ammunition. Hughes examines the crates.

LIEUTENANT HUGHES

You can fight an army with all this ammunition. Why so much?

TIMAR

Maybe they heard about my wife?

Hughes, puzzled, looks at Timar.

William kneels by his father's belongings. He shifts through the remains. Ragi walks up from behind.

WILLIAM MCLEOD

No bodies.

After a brief moment, the team reaches Ragi and William. Ragi addresses the team.

MAJOR RAGI

Look about. Look for clues.

Lucy stands before the spot the dead bodies were cremated.

LUCY

Ragi.

Ragi walks to Lucy.

LUCY

What does this mean?

MAJOR RAGI

I do not know.

William and Alan stand before a giant cage.

ALAN STUDWICK

Why on earth would they need this?

William shrugs his shoulders.

As the team investigate, Sihindi is seen standing on the outskirts of the camp.

SIHINDI

(whispers to herself)

More soldiers. More demons.

As the team probe, Sihindi stealthily moves in and attacks the team, using her martial art skills. She knocks down Alan and Rattan.

The "something", the beast, some distance away from Sihindi, senses Sihindi and roars.

Alan and Rattan lay on the ground. Sihindi knocks down Hughes. Jang and William rush Sihindi and pin her to the ground.

SIHINDI

Let me go you animals.

JANG SINGH

Calm.

WILLIAM MCLEOD

Who are you? Why do you attack us?

Sihindi breaks free and knocks Jang to the ground. As she does, she sees Jang's iron bracelet. She looks about and sees the bracelet on Rattan, Seva, Ragi, and Manh. She hesitates to throw another hit. She recognizes the iron bracelet as one of the five Ks of the Khalsa.

Just then, the beast, "the something", bursts through the trees. The expedition team are astonished and taken aback. The beast is a giant lion, black, the size of an adult Asian elephant, with piercing yellow eyes. The expedition team are in awe. The sight of this creature strikes fear, and simultaneously, amazes all the team members. This beast should not exist, yet, it does.

The lion charges the team, and as he does, Ragi rushes the lion with his sword in hand. The lion jumps into the air and Ragi slides underneath him, with his sword aimed at the lion's belly. The sword doesn't penetrate the lion's skin and shatters. The lion turns around and runs at Ragi. Ragi is able to move to one side without harm and grab the lion's mane. Ragi climbs onto the lion's back. Ragi hangs on for his life. The lion, attempting to shake off Ragi, runs into the jungle. Sihindi chases them and the team follow.

Ragi and the lion crash through the jungle, and then silence. Sihindi and the team catch up to Ragi and the lion. Ragi is pinned against a large tree and the lion moves in.

SIHINDI

(speaks to the lion)

Stop.

The lion turns his head and sees Sihindi.

SIHINDI

They will not harm you, or me.

Hughes slowly points his rifle at the beast. William places his hand on the barrel and gently pushes the rifle down.

WILLIAM MCLEOD

The beast is calming.

The beast moves toward Sihindi.

SIHINDI

Go now. Once dinner is ready, I will call you.

ALAN STUDWICK

Are we dinner?

Jang grins.

JANG SINGH

The creature is a vegetarian. If the stories are true.

SEVA SINGH

What stories?

JANG SINGH

This creature is hundreds of years old; brought into this world by virtue of her wrath. She is the lion's keeper.

SIHINDI

By the evil of empire builders. It is their wrath that gave life to him. What are you doing here?

WILLIAM MCLEOD

We are searching for my father and his team. Why did you stop?

SIHINDI

You are not who I thought you were.

SEVA SINGH

Who did you think we were?

SIHINDI

Soldiers, here to take.

(brief pause)

Lucky for you,

(grabs Seva's bracelet)

a true Sikh is one to be honoured. Are you true?

SEVA SINGH

I... I do not know?

Merritt stumbles forward through the foliage.

WILLIAM MCLEOD

Merritt!

William rushes to Merritt. Merritt collapses.

Hari

Most of the expedition team sit about a fire. Merritt, unconscious, lay close by. The camp is set where the team first saw Stoker's camp. Stoker's camp is seen in the back.

JANG SINGH

Her name is Sihindi and this all occurred over 150 years ago.

SEVA SINGH

Come on Jang, she is not that old.

JANG SINGH

The creature is the reason she still lives. I do not know how.

Sihindi is standing in the shadows listening to Jang.

SIHINDI

It is Hari's nature.

Most of those about the fire are momentarily startled.

JANG SINGH

Who is Hari?

SIHINDI

The creature you speak of.

MAJOR RAGI

Its skin is impenetrable.

SIHINDI

Yes. He cannot be killed.

WILLIAM MCLEOD

Is it immortal?

SIHINDI

No. All that exists perishes. He will too and with him, I.

Merritt wakes from his unconscious state.

JOHN MERRITT

William, is that you?

William rushes to Merritt.

WILLIAM MCLEOD

John. What happened? My father?

JOHN MERRITT

He's alive but his wounds are infected. He's with fever.

Merritt attempts to get up but falls back unconscious.

SIHINDI

I know where he is.

Sihindi leads William, Ragi, and Hughes to Stoker.

MAJOR RAGI

What did you mean, Hari's nature?

SIHINDI

To rejuvenate. He is able to emanate an energy that keeps the body young and strong.

WILLIAM MCLEOD

Why have you not helped my father?

SIHINDI

Why did your father bring a cage? Do you also desire to catch Hari?

WILLIAM MCLEOD

No.

MAJOR RAGI

We saw burnt bodies.

SIHINDI

It was that or leave them to the creatures.

MAJOR RAGI

What happened to them?

SIHINDI

Hari. They attacked him. By the time I arrived, it was too late.

Sihindi turns a corner.

SIHINDI

Here.

Sihindi points to a small opening in the mountain. William rushes past them all and toward the cave.

William quickly scans the cave and then rushes to his father who lay on the ground.

WILLIAM MCLEOD

Father.

Lord Stoker slowly opens his eyes.

LORD STOKER MCLEOD

William.

WILLIAM MCLEOD

You will be okay.

Ragi, Hughes, and Sihindi enter and stand at the entrance.

LORD STOKER MCLEOD

I cannot move.

Sihindi, conflicted, stares at Stoker. She then leaves the cave.

LIEUTENANT HUGHES

Should I follow her?

MAJOR RAGI

No. Let her go.

LIEUTENANT HUGHES

How do we get him back?

MAJOR RAGI

I do not know. If we move him, we might cause more harm.

A little pur is heard. All turn around. The lion enters and Sihindi follows. Sihindi moves past Hari and to Stoker.

SIHINDI

Lay here.

The lion makes his way to Stoker. William worries.

SIHINDI

Your father will be okay.

The lion lay beside Stoker. A white light emanates. All witness Stoker heal.

The Truth

Lucy, Aree, Timar, Manh, Seva, Rattan, and Merritt are in camp. Merritt rests. The others sit about and talk.

LUCY

The British are not the evil you believe they are.

RATTAN SINGH

Before annexation , there were more schools in Punjab, little poverty, higher morality, all religions were respected. This changed after the British took the Sikh Empire.

MANH SINGH

We are not the only who suffer. Half the world cries. The Irish, the African, the Aboriginals too hurt.

LUCY

Is there anything the British got right?

SEVA SINGH

I like the railroads, oh, and the attire. Hmm... Where can I find a suit and tie?

Rattan and Manh laugh, and the others follow. As they laugh, Ragi, Hughes, and William walk into camp. Stoker stops Sihindi before she and Hari enter.

LORD STOKER MCLEOD

If I may ask—Can your friend make me young?

SIHINDI

Yes. It requires Hari harness his energies for a year, and since the lion healed you...

LORD STOKER MCLEOD

I understand.

(brief pause)

My man Merritt, he is hurt. Can Hari heal him?

SIHINDI

Tell me the truth, why are you here?

LORD STOKER MCLEOD

The truth! You might not like the truth. I want my strength back. I want my youth back. I came to learn if the story of your lion is true.

SIHINDI

It is. Now what?

LORD STOKER MCLEOD

Now, I do not know. Perhaps I come back in a year.

SIHINDI

And what value is it to give you youth? Rich men are the reason India suffers. Rich men are the reason I lost everything. Can your money resurrect the dead?

William walks back for the two.

WILLIAM MCLEOD

Is everything okay?

LORD STOKER MCLEOD

Yes son. Sihindi and I were only talking.

Stoker walks into camp and William, Sihindi, and Hari follow. Sihindi sees Merritt. Sihindi turns to Hari.

SIHINDI

(as she strokes the lion's face)

Please help that man.

The lion moves to Merritt and nestles beside him.

Vegetarian

The morning sunlight is stunning. The air is fresh. The trees look beautiful. The birds sing gracefully.

Ragi and Hughes talk, William and Lucy flirt, Sihindi feeds Hari, and Stoker and Merritt converse.

MAJOR RAGI

There are no others. We leave for Lockhart soon.

LIEUTENANT HUGHES

Will there be a fort to return to?

MAJOR RAGI

(brief pause)

Let the others know.

LIEUTENANT HUGHES

Our intel was wrong.

MAJOR RAGI

We were lied to.

LIEUTENANT HUGHES

We need more men.

Sihindi feeds Hari a bread-like wrap with berries and greens inside. The red juices from the berries flow down the lion's face. Stoker and Merritt watch.

JOHN MERRITT

Can you believe that? How did it get so big eating only berries and greens?

LORD STOKER MCLEOD

Magic, Merritt. Magic.

JOHN MERRITT

I don't think we'll cage it.

Anagh Arrives

Anagh stands before the General, in the General's office.

GENERAL ANDREWS

Thank you Anagh. Captain, load all valuables and necessary documents. Send them to Delhi.

CAPTAIN FLECK

Shall I inform the forts?

GENERAL ANDREWS

Immediately.

There's a knock at the door.

GENERAL ANDREWS

Enter.

The secretary enters with Tristan.

GENERAL ANDREWS

Tristan, this might not be the ideal time.

TRISTAN JACOBS

I saw Anagh. Where are the others?

GENERAL ANDREWS

They should be at their destination. Anagh hurried back. More invaders than expected head this way.

Recruitment

Rattan, Jang, Manh, and Seva joke about and prepare to leave. As they do, Ragi approaches.

MAJOR RAGI

Jang, may I speak with you?

JANG SINGH

The answer is no.

MAJOR RAGI

I am yet to ask.

JANG SINGH

What do we care if the Afghans destroy a British fort.

MAJOR RAGI

If the fort falls, North India will be next.

Major Ragi walks away. Jang briefly ponders.

JANG SINGH

Men, we leave for Lockhart.

RATTAN SINGH

Jang! I will not go.

JANG SINGH

To live under British tyranny or an Afghanie hell? Which is better Rattan?

Rattan is angry.

JANG SINGH

(yells out to Ragi)

We will lead. We know a shortcut.

Ragi stops and turns around.

JANG SINGH

We require ammunition, and what about Sihindi and Hari?

Sihindi feeds Hari are not too far. Ragi approaches the two.

MAJOR RAGI

We require your help?

SIHINDI

No.

MAJOR RAGI

The invaders will overrun India.

SIHINDI

Hari and I will be fine.

MAJOR RAGI

I beg you, reconsider.

SIHINDI

I beg you, let us live in peace.

Major Ragi puts his head down and walks away. He heads toward Hughes, and soon after, he reaches Hughes, who's talking with Lord Stoker and Merritt.

MAJOR RAGI

Hughes, I need a hand with the Lord's ammunition.

JOHN MERRITT

The crates are intact?

MAJOR RAGI

Yes.

Stoker laughs.

LORD STOKER MCLEOD

It works. The crates were sprayed with a liquid that repels fire. I invented it.

LIEUTENANT HUGHES

Why so many?

LORD STOKER MCLEOD

Because there are never enough bullets when you need them.

Gold

Swami Faki and Grandpa Faki sit in chairs and enjoy tea, on the rooftop of their home.

SWAMI FAKI

Anagh did not.

GRANDFATHER FAKI

He is a gentle boy. Killing is not in his nature.

Charan enters and behind him is Captain Fleck.

GRANDFATHER FAKI

Ah, Captain. Sit. Have tea.

Fleck sits. Charan pours the Captain a cup of tea and hands it to him. Under Grandfather Faki's chair is a small chest.

GRANDFATHER FAKI

(as he taps the chest with his cane)

Charan, please place the chest on the table.

Charan places the chest on the table.

GRANDFATHER FAKI

Thank you for your past service. We have one last task. Please, open.

(gestures to the chest)

Fleck opens the chest and discovers it full of gold coins.

SWAMI FAKI

Hughes must die.

Heading Back

The team quickly move through the jungle. The rebels are on horseback. Jang leads. Ragi paces beside him.

JANG SINGH

We will be there by tomorrow afternoon.

MAJOR RAGI

Can you gather more men?

JANG SINGH

Yes.

MAJOR RAGI

Will you?

JANG SINGH

Manh is tasked with informing the others. As soon as we are close, he will get the word out.

The Afghans Arrive

The Afghans approach Lockhart. A British soldier on the wall spots the Afghans and sounds the alarm. The General rushes out of his office. Lockhart's main gate is closed. British soldiers hurry out of the armory, and others rush to man the cannons.

The General and Fleck stand on the fort wall and observe the enemy. The Waziristanis are establishing camp.

Hours pass by and the evening sets, and the Afghans are yet to attack.

LIEUTENANT HUGHES

Why do they not attack?

General Andrews remains silent.

Inside Ghazi Mirzali's Khan Wazir's tent, Raheed questions the Wazir.

RAHEED

Why do we wait? End this.

GHAZI MIRZALI KHAN WAZIR

Let the men rest. The more who rest, the less will die.

RAHEED

We have enough to spare.

GHAZI MIRZALI KHAN WAZIR

Understand this Raheed, every Muslim life matters. There is no difference between the rich and the poor in the eyes of Allah.

Raheed angrily leaves the tent.

It Begins

The sun rises. Afghanie horsemen, war elephants, cannons, and soldiers move into position.

General Andrews walks up the stairs and to the top of the fort wall. Captain Fleck is there observing the Afghans.

CAPTAIN FLECK

They have us surrounded.

An Afghan horseman rides toward Lockhart's main gate and stops close enough to be heard.

AFGHAN HORSEMAN

Surrender. Accept Islam. You will be spared.

After a brief moment, the General takes the rifle from Fleck's hand and shoots the Afghan horseman dead.

The Wazir is angry.

GHAZI MIRZALI KHAN WAZIR

Unleash the cannons.

The Afghan cannons fire at the fort.

GENERAL ANDREWS

Fire!

Fort Lockhart fires her cannons at the Afghans.

Almost There

The expedition team is trekking forward. Major Ragi stops.

MAJOR RAGI

Team, we rest here.

JANG SINGH

Manh, a quick break and then go.

MANH SINGH

Will do.

MAJOR RAGI

Once we arrive, we will be in the thick of it. Do what you must to prepare, and if you wish not to fight, now is the time to leave. There is no shame in this.

No person makes gestures to leave, and all go about preparing.

Alan cleans his rifle. Timar eats. Aree sits on top of a boulder and stares in the direction of the sun. Lucy sits at the base of the boulder and writes in her journal. Stoker and Merritt inspect their weapons. The Sikhs, excluding Manh, and William meditate.

Aree jumps up.

AREE

(Excited)

Repannon!

LUCY

What?

AREE

The size of a caboose.

Aree gets down from the boulder, packs her gear, and then yells out to Ragi.

AREE

Major, I have something that might help. It needs a little work but I can make it work.

Major opens his eyes. Aree jumps on a horse, belonging to Jang, and rides toward her home.

AREE

I will meet you at Lockhart.

Ragi looks about. Manh is fiddling with his rifle.

MAJOR RAGI

Manh Singh, please follow her. Keep her safe. Then leave for your men.

Manh looks at Jang. Jang nods his head in agreement. Manh packs his gear and rides after Aree.

MAJOR RAGI

(Ragi looks to Jang)

Thank you.

JANG SINGH

We should also be on our way.

Under Fire

Fort Lockhart is under attack and fighting back. The British battle hard. The General and Captain Fleck are on the wall and unloading bullets.

Fort Lockhart is firing everything at the invaders but the Afghans take light hits and slowly move forward.

CAPTAIN FLECK

Too many.

General Andrews continues to fire his rifle, and unknown to him, the team arrive behind the Afghans. Lucy, Seva, and Rattan are on horseback.

LIEUTENANT HUGHES

How should we hit them?

JANG SINGH

The way we always do. We quickly strike and we quickly move.

MAJOR RAGI

(short pause)

Okay. Lucy, Seva. Climb the highest trees. Shot anyone who gets close. Everyone else, follow Jang's lead.

From concealed positions, the team shoot at the right of the Afghans who attack the main gate. Many Afghans fall. The Afghans fire in the direction they were attacked from, but the team has moved on, and now stealthily assaults the center of the Afghans who attack the main gate. Again, Afghan soldiers fall, and again, the Afghans fire at the team but the team has moved on to attack the left of the Afghans. The Afghans again fall and fire back. Again, the team has moved on.

General Andrews notices the Afghans falling.

GENERAL ANDREWS

(as he fires his rifle)

We have help.

CAPTAIN FLECK

Who is it?

GENERAL ANDREWS

(as he fires his rifle)

I do not know.

The team again attack the center of the Afghan forces who attack the main gate. The Afghans take hits, but fire back quick enough that the team can't move to their next position. The team are pinned and hide from enemy fire.

Four Afghans stealthily approach the right of the team. Lucy and Seva spot them and snipe three down. Merritt takes down the fourth.

As the fourth Afghan falls, a large number of Afghans are seen moving toward the team.

TIMAR

This is it.

JANG SINGH

Have faith.

The Afghan soldiers are closing in on the team. Lucy and Seva fire as quickly as they can. The team on the ground fire. Many Afghans fall, but there are too many and the Afghans continue to move in.

Suddenly, tremendous amounts of gunfire lashes forward from the right of the Afghans. Within moments, most of the Afghans fall. Two dozen rebel Sikhs, including Manh Singh, slowly move forward from out the foliage, and join the team.

JANG SINGH

Waheguru Ji Ka Khalsa. Waheguru Ji Ke Fateh.

ALL SIKH REBELS

Waheguru Ji Ka Khalsa. Wahegur Ji Ke Fateh.

LORD STOKER MCLEOD

We need more guns or we are done.

The Repannon

Two elephants, pulling carts, move quickly. Aree rides the lead elephant, which transports the repannon. The repannon is covered by a large cloth. The other elephant, tied to the lead with a rope, carries the repannon's ammunition: small, baseball sized, cannon balls. Aree is almost in position.

The Afghans are on the verge of overtaking the team, when suddenly, the repannon's ammo flies by the Afghans and blasts apart trees and cracks boulders. The Afghans are in shock.

Aree is firing the repannon. The repannon is an automatic cannon that repeatedly fires small cannon balls, as a machine gun might. The repannon rests on the cart.

A few Afghans are hit by the repannon, and a few Afghans, on the sight of this, run.

LIEUTENANT HUGHES

Aree!

MAJOR RAGI

She has no defenders. We move to her.

The team rush toward Aree and take a defensive position around the repannon. All the Afghans before the repannon fall. Aree stops firing.

AREE

Help me reposition.

Aree jumps off the cart. The team reposition the repannon toward a large group of enemy soldiers. Aree gets behind the trigger and fires. The team also fire their rifles. All the Afghans fall.

The team reposition the cannon toward another group of Afghan soldiers. Aree fires. The team too fires. All the Afghans before them fall.

Night

Many hours of fighting lay waste and night has fallen.

AREE

NO MORE.

The repannon's ammunition is exhausted, and as it is, enemy soldiers move in. The team can't hold them back.

Suddenly, Hari, with Sihindi on his back, knock numerous Afghans to the ground as he rushes by. Hari then turns about and quickly pounces on enemy soldiers, one after another. Many Afghans, on witnessing Hari's fury, flee.

Afghan soldiers surrounding Fort Lockhart take notice of Hari. Crowds of soldiers are seen slowly moving toward Hari.

Captain Fleck is still on the wall top and his rifle is aimed at Hughes.

Hari and Sihindi watch the Afghan soldiers who gather to witness Hari. Hari lets out a massive roar. The Afghan soldiers turn and run. Hari pursues and destroys them.

The Wazir takes notice and positions his cannons on Hari. The cannons fire.

Hari is hit three times before falling. Sihindi doesn't let go off Hari.

The Wazir smiles and the soldiers surrounding him cheer. Yet, Hari quickly gets up, with Sihindi on his back, and runs toward the Wazir. The Wazir and his soldiers are shocked.

Captain Fleck fires his rifle and the bullet zooms by Hughes and takes out the Afghanie behind Hughes. The Afghanie was about to stab Hughes in the back.

Hari rushes the Wazir and his soldiers. Hari destroys the soldiers. Hari then, with his claw, hits the Wazir to the ground. Hari hovers over him for a brief moment before Sihindi dismounts and finishes the Wazir with her sword.

Morning After

Stoker, Tristan, and Merritt sit at the kitchen table, inside Mcleod's home. The package Tristan picked-up from the train station, when he first saw William, rests on the table. Dudley plays in the background. William enters the kitchen. Tristan opens the package and pulls out a new pair of prescription glasses. He calmly takes off his broken glasses and puts the new pair on.

WILLIAM MCLEOD

When do you leave?

LORD STOKER MCLEOD

Soon.

WILLIAM MCLEOD

Are you done with Kashmir?

LORD STOKER MCLEOD

For now.

WILLIAM MCLEOD

Let it go. I might not be there to rescue you next time.

(smirks)

LORD STOKER MCLEOD

I am proud of you son, and I know Tommy would be too.

TRISTAN JACOBS

Yes William, he would be amazed by you. We all are.

William is silent. He grabs a cup of tea and leaves for the backyard.

William makes his way to a tree in the far back of the yard and sits underneath the tree. He's in deep thought. His teacup rests beside him. As William ponders, a pebble hits him. William looks about but sees no person. Another pebble hits him. William looks up and into the tree.

TOMMY

Hi William.

William gets up.

WILLIAM MCLEOD

Tommy! What? How?

TOMMY

Hari. He's a healer.

The night that Hari healed Merritt, as all slept, Hari also healed William's mind.

WILLIAM MCLEOD

But how are you here?

TOMMY

I watch you. You are good. I mean, you never miss with your rifle, and your punch, it can knock down a bull.

William looks down.

TOMMY

It is okay, you know. It was time for me to go. And William, it is amazing here. I'm happy; happier than ever before.

Tommy hangs onto the branch he was sitting on and swings to the ground. William looks at Tommy.

TOMMY

I want you to be happy, like me.

Suddenly, a loud bang is heard. William turns to look. Tristan is on the ground. William runs to Tristan.

WILLIAM MCLEOD

Tristan!

TRISTAN JACOBS

I am okay. Were you talking with someone?

William looks back but doesn't see Tommy. William walks back to where Tommy was and looks about. Tristan follows.

TRISTAN JACOBS

What is it?

WILLIAM MCLEOD

The end of a chapter.

Wrap-Up

It's the afternoon and hot, and the day following the siege on Fort Lockhart. Major Ragi roams the Peshawar Bazaar. He seeks the spy who lied about the number of invading Afghans. Ragi spots him, chases him down, and places him under arrest.

A week later, Fleck, with a dozen British soldiers, arrives at the Faki home and arrests the Fakis.

SWAMI FAKI

What? What is this?

CAPTAIN FLECK

A plot to murder a British soldier; it is a line you should not have crossed.

Swami Faki and Grandpa Faki are arrested.

One month later Hughes and Nadira marry, in the traditional Indian style.

Two months later Lucy has a book release, and William is there, holding her hand.

Three months later, at the Sikh rebel camp, Seva opens a box and finds European attire. Seva is excited. He shows the others. The others about him laugh.

Four months after the battle at Lockhart, Aree works in her shop and finalizes her new invention. Ragi comes from behind her and holds her. Aree smiles and continues her work.

On the other side of the world, Alan Studwick sails his new ship.

And as for Hari and Sihindi, they both live in peace in the Kashmir jungle. For now.

MORE ADVENTURE TO COME.

Appendix A: The Khalsa

Sometimes, a noble army rises. Sometimes, the righteous ones come together and battle the wicked. Among the Sikh people can be found such an organization, and amid them is the greatest covenant of the past 1000 years, the Khalsa. Established in 1699 by the Great Gobind Singh, the Khalsa is an armed union that exists for the purpose of defending against all tyrannical powers, protecting dharma, and protecting the holy of all religions—without taking anything in return. To this effect, death is a companion of the Singh (a member of the Khalsa). There is no compromising. Puran Singh, a renowned Sikh academic writes in his book, Spirit of the Sikh:

> *"Death, apparent death, is embraced by The Khalsa as no lover ever embraced his sweetheart. The Khalsa dies like the dashing waves of the sea, creating in the wake of its death millions more like itself. The life-breath of The Khalsa thus is losing its apparent life to gain its life everlasting."*

> *"In the ideal of The Khalsa, one can see the Ideal spirit of the passionate love of death for the sale of life as is seen in the Bushido of the Samurai of Old Japan. In that fervour of Yamoto, the physical life turns all into a little moth flickering its wings in infinite impatience to die. Death is the bride of the brave."*

Max Arthur McAuliffe, in his book, The Sikh Religion: Volume 1, writes, *"...no superiority of the enemies in number, no shot, no shell, can make his heart quail, since his Amrit (baptism) binds him to fight single-handed against millions."* Rightfully so, the tyrants of the world are as strong as a million giants, and those brave enough to stand against them like the Biblical "David". Only without fear, and a will to sacrifice everything worldly, can the giants be defeated.

Not only is the Khalsa a community of warriors, the Khalsa is also a community of saints. Each member is humble, kind, gentle, loving, peaceful, fearless, forgiving, God-oriented, communally aware, soft-spoken, rational, truthful, mentally disciplined, knowledgeable, poetic, worldly, and detached from the self and Maya. The Khalsa only unsheathes the sword as a shield and not for secular gain. Puran Singh once wrote:

> *"Once it is said The Khalsa occupied the throne of Delhi when the Mughal Emperor submitted and acknowledged the power of The Khalsa, the leader Jassa Singh said—'Ah! The Khalsa is atit (untouched by Maya). What has it to do with thrones'—and gave the throne back to the Mughals."*

> *"No one need be afraid of The Khalsa of Guru Gobind Singh, that it would ever think of seeking the bones of material objects. The eyes of The Khalsa are fixed heavenward."*

As dictated by Guru Gobind Singh to the great Sikh scholar, Bhai Nand Lal Goya, Goya writes in his book, Tankhahnama:

> *"The Khalsa is he who protects the poor, who destroys the wicked, who recites the Name, who fights the enemy, who concentrates his mind on the Name, who is detached from all other ties, who rides the horse, who fights every day, who bears arms, who promotes dharam, and who dies for his faith."*

The famous Sikh historian, Rattan Singh Bhangu, writes in his book, Pracheen Panth Prakash, the following on the Khalsa's creation.

> *"The perfect Guru, the Tenth, created the Khalsa Panth in this manner, so that they must wage a war against oppression."*

Guru Gobind Ji further describes the Khalsa as *"he is whose heart burns unflickering the Lamp of Naam, day and night, know him the Khalsa, the pure!"* As recorded by Puran Singh.

This connection to the essence of God is the reason the Khalsa's history is full of Singhs able to overcome incredible odds and achieve superhuman deeds, akin to those performed by Banda Singh, Deep Singh, Hari Singh, and Jassa Singh. As the Jedi draws power from the Force, the Singh draws power from the Lamp of Naam (the Primal Energy that pervades within all known and unknown).

An 18th century Muslim historian, and an enemy of the Sikhs, Qazi Nur Mohammad, once wrote of the Khalsa and the Khalsa's spirit:

> *"Do not call the Sikhs dogs, because they are lions and are courageous like lions in the battlefield. How can a hero, who roars like a lion be called a dog? Like lions they spread terror in the field of battle. If you wish to learn the art of war, come face to face with them in the battlefield. They will demonstrate it to you in such a way that one and all will shower praise on them. If you wish to learn the science of war, O swordsman, learn from them. They advance at the enemy boldly and come back safely after action. Understand; Singh is their title, a form of address for them. It is not justice to call them dogs; if you do not know Hindustani language, then understand that the word 'Singh' means a lion.*
>
> *Truly, they are lion in battle, and at times of peace, they surpass in generosity. When they take the Indian sword in their hands they traverse the country from Hind to Sind. None can stand against them in battle, howsoever strong he may be. When they handle the spear, they shatter the ranks of the enemy. When they raise the heads of their spears towards the sky, they would pierce even through the Caucasus. When they adjust the strings*

of the bows, place in them the enemy killing arrows and pull the strings to their ears, the body of the enemy begins to shiver with fear. When their battle axes fall upon the armour of their opponents, their armour becomes their coffin.

The body of every one of them is like a piece of rock and in physical grandeur every one of them is more than fifty men. It is said that Behram Gore killed wild asses and lions. But if he were to come face to face with them even he would bow before them. Besides usual arms, they take their guns in hand and come into the field of action jumping and roaring like lions and raise slogans. They tear asunder the chests of many and shed blood of several in the dust. You say that musket is a weapon of ancient times, it appears to be a creation of these dogs rather than Socrates. Who else than these dogs can be adept in the use of muskets. They do not bother even if there are innumerable muskets. To the right and the left, in front and towards the back, they go on operating hundreds of muskets angrily and regularly.

...Besides their fighting, listen to one more thing in which they excel all other warriors. They never kill a coward who is running away from the battlefield. They do not rob a woman of her wealth or ornaments whether she is rich or a servant. There is no adultery among these dogs, nor are they mischievous people... There is no thief amongst these dogs, nor is there amongst them any mean people. They do not keep company with adulaters'... Now that you have familiarised yourself with the behaviour of the Sikhs, you may also know something about their country. They have divided Punjab amongst themselves and have bestowed it upon every young and old." — Jang Namah (1765)

Jang Namah is an eye-witness account of Ahmed Shah Durrani's invasion of Punjab, in the year 1764. Commissioned by Ahmed Shah, the author naturally compromises objectivity when describing events and the people the Afghans invaded. When reading his work, it's clear Nur Mohammed held a strong prejudice toward the Sikhs. He refers to them as dogs, dirty idolaters, fire worshippers, etc. Nevertheless, even with his biases, he was unable to prevent his pen from glorifying the Khalsa and the Khalsa's members.

Jang Namah also shares the story of Baba Gurbakhsh Singh Shaheed and the 30 Singhs who battled 30 000 Afghanies. The 31 fought to prevent the desecration of the Golden Temple.

The true Singh, a replica of Gobind, is able to harness Naam because those who serve the Khalsa serve God. The Khalsa is a union of the Pure (the spiritually liberated), and sanctioned by The Lord for the purpose of ushering in the "Kingdom of God". An era on earth the Singhs call the "Khalsa Raj", in which God, truth, equality, justice, freedom, and righteousness prevail. It's said that so long as the Singh is true to the principles of the Khalsa, God will protect the Singh. However, The Great Architect is quick to abandon those who forget.

According to author, Narain Singh, in his book, Guru Gobind Singh Re-told, a year prior to the creation of the Khalsa, Guru Gobind withdrew into the Naina Devi Hills to meditate. He sought to connect with God and request The Eternal's guidance. He was troubled by the fact that he was forced to resort to violence to combat violence. He was aware that aggression is an evil which destroys human values and an idea that contradicts the core teachings of Sikhie—love and non-violence. However, the Mughal Administration, in their quest to convert all of India to Islam, unleashed hell on the people of Hindustan. Only those who unsheathed the sword were able to retain their non-Islamic identity. Guru Gobind unsheathed out of necessity, and even though each battle resulted in his victory, he fully recognized that violence is unbecoming.

Gobind eventually united with The Formless One, and after his union, Gobind proclaimed, as written in his book, Bachittar Natak:

> *"The Lord has sent me into the world for the purpose of spreading Dharma. He said to me, 'Go and spread Dharma (righteousness) everywhere, seize and smash the evil doers.' Know ye holy men, I have come solely for the purpose of bringing about Dharma, saving holy men and completely uprooting wicked men."*

After his union, Guru Gobind established the Khalsa and initiated the quest to restore the conditions of an honourable existence. Conceived as a champion of dharma, the Khalsa is sanctioned by The Eternal to unsheathe but only in the face of extreme evil, and when peace is useless.

Sometimes, a noble army rises. Sometimes, the righteous ones come together and battle the wicked. Among the Sikh people can be found such an organization, and amid them is the greatest covenant of the past 1000 years, the Khalsa. Established in 1699 by the Great Gobind Singh, the Khalsa is an armed union that exists for the purpose of defending against all tyrannical powers, protecting dharma, and protecting the holy of all religions—without taking anything in return. To this effect, death is a companion of the Singh. There is no compromising.

> *"Says Kabeer, those humble people become pure - they become Khalsa - who know the Lord's loving devotional worship."* — Ang 655 of 1430, Sri Guru Granth Sahib Ji

Books by Mike

www.ingramcontent.com/pod-product-compliance
Lightning Source LLC
Chambersburg PA
CBHW030623310726
48979CB00003B/859
* 9 7 8 1 7 7 4 8 1 4 9 5 6 *